Mrs. Baul
Investigates

Mrs. Baul Investigates

Bishop Kidnapped in Egypt

LYNNE E. CHANDLER

iUniverse, Inc.
Bloomington

**Mrs. Baul Investigates
Bishop Kidnapped in Egypt**

Copyright © 2012 by Lynne E. Chandler.

All rights reserved. No part of this book may be used or reproduced by any means, graphic, electronic, or mechanical, including photocopying, recording, taping or by any information storage retrieval system without the written permission of the publisher except in the case of brief quotations embodied in critical articles and reviews.

iUniverse books may be ordered through booksellers or by contacting:

iUniverse
1663 Liberty Drive
Bloomington, IN 47403
www.iuniverse.com
1-800-Authors (1-800-288-4677)

Because of the dynamic nature of the Internet, any web addresses or links contained in this book may have changed since publication and may no longer be valid. The views expressed in this work are solely those of the author and do not necessarily reflect the views of the publisher, and the publisher hereby disclaims any responsibility for them.

Any people depicted in stock imagery provided by Thinkstock are models, and such images are being used for illustrative purposes only.
Certain stock imagery © Thinkstock.

ISBN: 978-1-4759-5061-8 (sc)
ISBN: 978-1-4759-5062-5 (ebk)

Printed in the United States of America

iUniverse rev. date: 09/20/2012

Contents

1. Banana Bishop rumblings 1
2. The stage is set 9
3. The players 15
4. Donkey Rescue 27
5. The threat 36
6. The Rt. Rev. Edwin Cornwall-McGrath III 46
7. The painting 53
8. Family reconnaissance 60
9. The explosion 71
10. The papyrus message 77
11. Joe disappears 82
12. Coastal developments 98
13. Donkey carts 109
14. Pursuit of the bishop 122
15. The mysterious illness of Madame Napoleon 131
16. The stalking journalist 141
17. Camels and pigeons 152
18. Magnoon Abdu 164
19. Espionage at large 174
20. Tracking trails of sand 183
21. Mrs. Baul digs deeper 193
22. The silencing of Mrs. Baul 200
23. News of Bishop Edwin 208
24. Racing terrorists home 216
25. The fate of Cinnamon and Sugar 225

To my parents,

Jack & Theo Robinson

"Gifts for the journey"

Acknowledgements

My thanks to . . .

*Auntie Dot - with deep admiration;
I wish I could have
shared this story with you*

*Paul-Gordon, Britelle, and Treston -
my family and life's inspiration*

*Dad and Mom -
for all your support and encouragement*

*Tom -
childhood adventurer, dear brother, friend*

*Robert Twigger -
brilliant writer, generous friend*

-1-

Banana Bishop rumblings

Mrs. Baul jolted awake to the mosque call vibrating from the newly installed speakers next door. Mistaking the culprit for an alarm clock her husband had bought her as a gift one year, she smiled to herself and relaxed once more. She had at least another hour. Rev. Baul turned toward her and mumbled contentedly as he entwined his hand in hers and drifted off again. That prayer reminder must have been woven into his dream.

But wait. That voice. It was definitely not the regular call of the *muezzin*. Something was awry.

"Sweetheart, something's wrong!" she shook her husband repeatedly and fumbled for the light switch.

"What is it? The same nightmare, darling?" Rev. Baul replied with as cheerful a voice as he could muster at this dark hour.

"No, it's the voice!" she whispered with slow panic creeping toward her chest.

"The voice?"

"The mosque caller! He's off tune!" she cried.

"Off tune?" Rev. Baul struggled to a sitting position, trying to make sense of his wife's distress.

"Yes, it's not the usual voice," she explained urgently. "We've had the same *muezzin* for five years! They've put in a spy!"

"Oh, goodness," calmed Rev. Baul. "I'm sure there's a simple explanation, my love. Maybe they've changed to a recorded voice, as so many mosques are these days."

"But it's dreadful," moaned Mrs. Baul trying to compose her quivering voice. "I'm sorry to be so sensitive. You know the minaret purposely peers right in our window. It's just too much for me sometimes."

"Why don't I go around tomorrow morning and get the full story?"

Mrs. Baul switched off the light and tried desperately to relax once more. Her mind was racing as she told herself to breathe in, breathe out, to rest in the moment and let go of her anxiety.

Light peered into their eyes an hour later and officially called them to the day. The flutter and cooing of Rev. Baul's undomesticated pigeon *Farrouk* drew him from his slumber. The bird's long royal feathered feet balanced precariously on the edge of the window box outside, waiting for seed to appear. Mrs. Baul loved to see her husband's connection with nature. Imagine a man of his standing and responsibility and yet he takes time to admire and care for creation.

Today promised to be busy so she really needed to get herself moving. Well, maybe in just another minute. Their household staff wouldn't be arriving for a while yet, but really all Rev. Baul had to do was press one button and the coffee she'd remembered to put in the machine before bed would be brewing. Cardamom flavored today; he would be pleased his favorite brand was back on the shelves of the corner market.

The weekly Holy Communion service for expatriates had gone well last night. Acolytes had arrived on time to serve, and freshly made bread and new candlesticks from the Coptic monastery had been delivered as promised. Because the regular accompanist had called in sick, Mrs. Baul had accompanied the choir with the historic Edinburgh organ. With only a slight mistake in her interpretation of Handel's *Sarabande* during the Offertory, Rev. Baul had graciously admired her beautiful playing afterwards.

She was sure he exaggerated the importance of her contributions, but she smiled appreciatively. The vocal talents of their teenage daughter Miriam were much more vital to setting the tone for worship. But of course their Joseph played the role of junior verger very efficiently too. Processional cross, robes, Gospel: all in place for Rev. Baul each Saturday evening. Since they lived in the Middle East it only made sense to respect the Muslim weekend and join the Friday/Saturday routine.

Now Sunday morning, the week was beginning anew: children to be delivered to school, charity events and coffees to attend, oh, and Book Club this morning. Mrs. Baul leaned over to her bedside table and scribbled herself a reminder.

"Good morning, my love," Rev. Baul greeted her with a glass of freshly squeezed orange juice. "Thank you for the good pot of coffee this morning," he said as he kissed her generously.

"Of course." Mrs. Baul's wistful hazel eyes met her husband's gaze as she drank down her juice and revived a bit. "I'm so sorry about disrupting your sleep this morning."

"No problem at all," he smiled back at her. "I will pop round to the mosque as I promised and get the full story. I wouldn't mind seeing if they could turn the volume down a notch or two either."

"Thank you, sweetheart," she replied. "What's your schedule like today?"

"Well, I have a meeting this morning about a new charity, Donkey Rescue, I think the man said," replied Rev. Baul vaguely as he set up his shaving supplies.

Mrs. Baul froze for a brief moment before nodding cheerfully and slipping off to see to the children's lunches. Her thoughts were not what they should be: still blurry after the scare with the call to prayer episode. This was the first mention she had heard about such a charity. Wasn't she, not her husband, always the point of contact for local charities? He was far too busy hosting visiting dignitaries and interfaith endeavors.

What in the world was a donkey rescue? It sounded like Rev. Baul was getting in over his head again. Donkeys. Rescue. Oh dear. Could it be some kind of code name? It would need time to sort out. Madame Napoleon was hosting the book club this morning. In light of her web of high connections and all, it would be wise to run such a development by her.

Book club was lively that morning. Happily, Mrs. Baul's contribution of homemade cinnamon rolls was ardently praised. Only Madame Napoleon seemed to pick up on the significance of the mosque-call incident. Discussion inevitably diverted to topics of general interest, the latest being the rumored disappearance of a bishop in Egypt's bordering country, Libya.

"That's funny, Rev. Baul hasn't mentioned it. Our Egyptian bishop oversees that province. When did this happen?" asked Mrs. Baul quite confused and a bit put out that she wasn't the one to be making such an announcement. "Where was he from?"

"Just breaking news this morning," explained Madame Napoleon as she adjusted her glasses on her long protruding nose. "From somewhere in South America, I think; sold plantation bananas to the Libyan government in addition to his role as a visiting dignitary."

Sold bananas? A bishop? That didn't sound very likely. Who was that bishop they'd met during their Tunisian posting? Cobwebs. That was even before Grandpa Baul had moved in with them and Mrs. Baul's stress levels had increased significantly.

Rev. Baul was working as the Vicar of the historic St. George's Church then. Their vicarage garden had sheltered the Red Cross during the North Africa Campaign. Commemorative plaques lined the walls of the building and graves dotted the church garden. Mrs. Baul had flourished in Tunis with all the charity opportunities the British Ambassador had kindly sent her way: orphanage visits, fundraising luncheons, and the support of environmental causes. Yes, that was also the patch of time Mrs. Baul's suspicious mind had successfully begun to link together years of subtle clues as to the full identity of her beloved husband.

Mrs. Baul had often dreamed of the exotic life of being married to an "agent" long before she had met Rev. Baul. Growing up in the Ituri Forest of central Africa with parents who were anthropologists had opened the door to such employment ideas. Her friends, many of whom were Bantu pygmies, had taught her the patient skills of tracking for information.

One year some misinformed rebels had surrounded their village, convinced that the leprosarium was a cover for foreign operatives. Tragically, a close friend her age was killed accidentally in a crossfire battle. Those images were never successfully pushed out of her heart or mind, a trauma only shared with her husband, and even then exposing the rawness of her pain very briefly. Years later she still found herself unable to watch war movies or read books with violent or traumatic themes. Mrs. Baul thought such undercover employment extremely implausible, yet the sense of adventure often lured her daydreams and the desire to face her own fears and help others in danger tugged at her almost unconsciously.

When Rev. Baul first swept her off her feet, she had had no inclination he was involved in fulfilling such a dream. Time had aged her husband well. Still as handsome as ever, she loved to run her fingers through his slightly graying hair. His medium height fit hers perfectly and she never ceased to melt at the warm display of his generous dimples.

Mrs. Baul's first inkling to her husband's possible double identity had surfaced in Tunisia ten years earlier. In addition to being the Vicar, for passport visa-granting purposes Rev. Baul was in the country with the title of Chaplain to the British Ambassador. One evening Rev. Baul returned from his monthly "confessional" debriefing with the ambassador and confidentially reported a very telling conversation. Mrs. Baul could still remember the discussion as if it were yesterday.

"I had an interesting meeting with the ambassador today," Rev. Baul reported to his wife. "He asked me to assist the MI6 in their worldwide mission."

"You mean like 007?" Mrs. Baul gasped.

"Well, he didn't put it in those words of course," her husband clarified. "When I turned him down he warned me that our conversation had never taken place, strictly off the record and bound to the confines of confessional confidentiality."

"You turned him down?" Mrs. Baul thought perhaps she'd heard incorrectly.

"Of course, I am American by birth and by passport and so I will remain," he replied emphatically.

"I wonder why he was trying to recruit you?" she probed further.

"I'm sure the fact that I've spoken French and Arabic fluently since my childhood in Muslim West Africa is attractive," he explained. "And he alluded to my current position as a priest as the sort of cover he could only dream of, although in my mind I question the ethics."

"I see," noted his wife in a way that marked her disapproval of brushing off the proposal so quickly.

"Anyway, how could I possibly fulfill my writing dreams and produce a spiritually and intellectually filled sermon each week with too many irons in the fire?"

"I'm sure the best of ministers could not, sweetheart, but you are exceptionally gifted," encouraged Mrs. Baul.

"Please don't breathe a word of this to anyone else my love," asked Rev. Baul. "I just tell you in the strictest confidence as my wife and confidant."

"Of course," his wife nodded compliance.

The conversation ended abruptly at that point and it was the sole time it was ever mentioned. Mrs. Baul knew her husband could do anything he set his mind to with passion and ample energy. She mulled over this event, the offer, for months. Without daring to get someone else's opinion, the only conclusion she could reach was that Rev. Baul was already working undercover. He had brightness in his spirit that was a successful recipe for fanning the divine spark in others and celebrating life abundantly.

Mrs. Baul's mind opened to a flood of memories and "proofs." For one, there was the incident when Mrs. Baul's dish gloves had gone missing. The maid's discovery of the incriminating evidence as she dusted the desk of Rev. Baul was initially quite a shock. Mrs. Baul had thought of confronting him at the time but realized it would put future reconnaissance opportunities in jeopardy. It had been a wise decision.

Many things had happened since then; clandestine activities that an eye less gifted would overlook. The thirst for adventure and purpose in the unpretentious spirit of Mrs. Baul began to blossom.

-2-

The stage is set

Grandpa Baul awoke a bit out of sorts that morning. After hearing the neighborhood mosque's call to prayer, he stretched his tall narrow frame and drifted back into a shallow sleep, as he mulled over the remaining problem preventing the completion of his latest invention.

He would miss his run to the *wadi*, dry riverbed, just outside town; traffic would have picked up by then. It must have been the early hours of the morning before he'd given up looking for proof of his theory and retired to bed. The project was at a standstill. Best if he ran his thoughts past the kids after school anyway. Joe could do some final adjustments on the computer program he was designing. Plenty of other work awaited his attention.

Was today the maid's scheduled visit to clean his garden guesthouse quarters? She knew how to preserve his creations and still scare away the dust. He must remember to compliment his son on a sermon well done last night, tactfully of course if his daughter-in-law was present. She could twist a compliment into something subversive without ever realizing what she was doing. He had sat through more sermons than he could count; he knew an exceptional one when he heard it. Grandpa Baul's wife had been witnessing those sermons from Heaven now for nearly ten years. He still missed her presence deeply.

Now daily life for Grandpa revolved around his two grandchildren, and the setup here was ideal. When he thought of his friends retiring back in the States and forced into routines of leisure he just shook his head with thankfulness at his good luck. At first his son had refused to entertain the thought of his living in the old servants' quarters in the back of the garden. However, continual access to his workshop and guaranteed privacy for meetings was a necessity. With a bit of encouragement from his persuasive children, Rev. Baul slowly came round to their way of thinking.

Mrs. Baul had certainly displayed her share of unusual behavior since his arrival on the scene, but the goodness in her passion for helping others usually outweighed the frustration of her eccentricities. His son doted on her excessively but happily, so why disturb his equilibrium? Miriam and Joe saw things his way. They loved their mother dearly and certainly worked hard to keep her out of harm's way.

By midday, Mrs. Baul was certain that this missing Banana Bishop was not at all who Madame Napoleon had reported him to be. Case of mistaken identity to be sure: perhaps a screen to keep the real situation under rap. Bishop Kareem here in Cairo may know more. What if he was tangled up in this mess himself? Rev. Baul would most assuredly know the details before the day's finish, and perhaps she could probe discretely.

Had he mentioned any recent visits from the Rt. Rev. Edwin Cornwall-McGrath III? That was certainly a possibility. His Grace had been seated as a bishop in Chichester, England where Rev. Baul had been recruited for seminary. Since then they had witnessed his rise to Advisor of the Archbishop of Canterbury. He was currently negotiating inter-religious dialogue on a worldwide scale. Gradually Mrs. Baul began to piece things together.

Hadn't Bishop Edwin been the one to invite Rev. Baul to the late night soirees with the famous author and Nobel Prize winner, Naguib Mafouz? What about those lunches with the sheikhs at Al-Azhar, the intellectual seat of Sunni Islam worldwide?

Mrs. Baul wondered if she could lay hands on one of those black head-to-toe outfits and do a bit of sleuthing herself. She must ask her Arabic tutor what they were called—specifically the ones with the screened eyes: that would be perfect. Miriam would know the name, but then questions would arise. Of course, Madame Napoleon alone held the solution.

No, Mrs. Baul would need less traditional methods to satisfy her curiosity. The whole affair could prove far too dangerous without a full complement of gadgets or back-up agents at her disposal. She would not risk the intrusion of potential danger or harmful repercussions upon her family.

Well, musings these thoughts would have to remain. A parishioner needed visiting and then on to her last coffee appointment of the day before dashing to pick up the children from school. Or had Grandpa Baul said he would handle that today? Her plate was too full. And what of this Donkey Rescue business?

Well, if it wasn't the striking blue eyes of Rev. Baul that met her as she entered their favorite café. Mrs. Baul's heart skipped a beat; he was sitting with another woman she had never seen before. Or had she? Rev. Baul seemed equally surprised to see her, but delighted rather than put out. Perhaps there wasn't a hidden agenda in progress after all. And for goodness sakes, no well-trained agent in their right mind would speak in such a public location full of planted listening ears. Speaking of listening ears, Mrs. Baul spotted the infamous "listener" of their church, Felix the Spy.

The church had never been told his full name so Felix it was. In a land where every other male seemed to bear the name Ahmed or Muhammed it was a very strange name indeed to choose as an alias. Felix was quite harmless though. Following a church service one evening, Mrs. Baul put all apprehension aside and convinced her children to join in a covert attempt to follow Felix and discover his secret headquarters. She explained it would be best if her suspicions were kept from the ears of Grandpa Baul and their father. Unfortunately, as Mrs. Baul was driving their car and Felix was riding an old bicycle, the scouting mission was thwarted by traffic within two blocks of the church.

All these images flashed through Mrs. Baul's mind in milliseconds as she composed herself and walked in a dignified and unrushed manor over to greet Rev. Baul. His dimples deepened and his blue eyes actually twinkled as she approached; her elevated heart rate quickly subsided.

"Hello my love," her husband called as she approached his table.

"Hi sweetheart," answered Mrs. Baul with only a slight tone of uneasiness in her voice.

"Mrs. Baul," the woman wearing the bright red hat whirled around to greet her as well.

Oh goodness, Mrs. Baul had not recognized the new hat of the church treasurer. Sensing relief that nothing out of the ordinary was in progress, Mrs. Baul greeted them warmly and moved on toward a corner table to join Madame Napoleon. These two women made a very unique pair. Madame, tall and solidly built, had high cheekbones and dark brown eyes. Mrs. Baul, although shorter, displayed a collection of freckles rather than wrinkles, wide set hazel eyes and straight white teeth when she smiled.

"I must speak to you," whispered Mrs. Baul.

"What is it?" Madame Napoleon mirrored her sense of urgency.

"Have you ever heard of a Donkey Rescue here in Cairo?" Mrs. Baul queried.

"Well, now we used to have something of the sort in Jerusalem. I don't know off the top of my head. Why?" she asked.

"Oh, I was just wondering. A certain someone mentioned it might be part of our church's charity fundraising program this year but I had never heard of it, until this week," she explained.

"That is a bit odd. You of all people would know if a legitimate new charity had been launched in Cairo. Let me ask around discretely," she suggested. "We're hosting another reception tonight. Many connection opportunities, if you know what I mean."

This would not be the first time Mrs. Baul and Madame Napoleon had joined forces. Both were admired for charity work in their respective fields, Madame being the wife of the Ambassador of the European Union in Egypt. Raised in London but Egyptian by birth, Madame Napoleon was delighted when her French husband gave her the opportunity to live in the country of her ancestors. She and Mrs. Baul had moved to Cairo the same summer and become inseparable friends.

-3-

The players

Grandpa Baul picked up Miriam and Joe from school as scheduled. The American international school they attended reflected a wide variety of nationalities. This year the "back to school night" had reported 65 different countries represented. In addition to a sound education his grandchildren were getting to mingle alongside creeds and cultures that mirrored the United Nations.

Today the security guards allowed him to drive right up near the entrance to wait. His daughter-in-law would not have approved of such lax security. Well-trained German Shepherds sat in the shade panting and looking bored. The head of security knew Grandpa Baul by name now and gave a friendly salute in greeting. Their last encounter had been a result of Mrs. Baul's official complaint about a new decorative sculpture installed outside the front gate. Certain that terrorists would use it to mount the wall of her children's educational compound, she had arranged one meeting after another until grudgingly convinced that her fear was unfounded.

"Hi Grandpa!" called Joe as he emerged from the walled school gates minutes later.

"Hey Joe!" replied Grandpa, always proud to see his tall muscular grandson with an entourage of girls at his side. He had his father's dimples but his mother's striking eyes.

"Miriam is just buying the supplies you asked for at the school store," Joe explained.

"Well done. How was your day?" Grandpa's cloudy blue eyes welcomed him happily from behind a new pair of glasses.

"Fine. Hey, I like your glasses, Grandpa. They're cool," praised Joe. "They look good with your white hair."

"Thanks Joe," smiled Grandpa. "You had band today, right?"

"Yeah, last period. I really like that new instrument strap you made me. The ergonomics of that Neotech stuff is awesome," Joe said enthusiastically.

"Oh good. No sense getting sore neck muscles from a tenor saxophone. Sorry I had to borrow the mouthpiece. Don't think I damaged it though. Did it play smoothly enough?" Grandpa Baul queried.

"Yeah, no problem," Joe nodded.

"Hey Miriam!" Grandpa shouted out the window to his granddaughter when she appeared at last. She too seemed to have an admiring escort. With wavy brown hair, her father's clear blue eyes, and her mother's warm smile she was a knockout.

"Hi Grandpa! Love your new glasses," Miriam said admiringly. "I bet you got some random good looking lady at the store to help you pick those out."

"You know me well," Grandpa teased back.

"I hardly have any homework," Miriam continued. "Can we go felucca sailing? Please?"

"What do you think, Joe? Do you have time? I'm guessing your mom will be back within an hour or so," Grandpa explained.

"I can bring my laptop. I just have to study for a math test later but it's going to be easy. Miriam do you want to try out the *hijaab*?" asked Joe.

"Does it feel like a real headscarf yet or just look like one?" asked Miriam

"Well, I guess it is sort of stiff, but once we get the electronic threads and the earpiece right we can worry about style," Grandpa's contagious laugh got them all going. Leave it to Grandpa. "Hey, I'm a little worried about your mom again. Your dad was dropping subtle hints at lunch that she was a bit distracted. He's probably guessing she needs another vacation."

"Oh boy, here we go again," Joe rolled his eyes.

"Hey, in World Cultures today we were talking about a missing bishop in Libya. It's major international news. I wonder if Dad knows anything more? I sure hope Mom's not going there. Can you imagine the kind of trouble she could get him into?" Miriam didn't need to elaborate.

They all went home and grabbed what they needed before heading to the Nile. Best if they left a note welcoming their mother back from her busy day and ensuring her they were safely in the presence of their grandfather.

Prior to Rev. Baul's announcement of the move to Egypt, mayhem had reigned briefly in the sensitive mind of Mrs. Baul the day her traveling husband reported home

from an overseas "business trip," as he labeled it. Long had she wondered as to the exact nature of his work. Moving every few years from country to country and job to job was regarded as a normal way of life. She would not have questioned the routine, proudly seeing herself as a sort of goodwill ambassadress at large.

Daydreams, being what they are, often allowed her mind free reign to explore the realm of her important role in the world, perhaps a cross between Mother Teresa and 007? Not that fame was important to her. Making a contribution in the world; that was her slogan and she drummed the theme into the growing minds and hearts of her two young children.

She remembered the dooming conversation as if it was yesterday.

"Cairo, Egypt has 22 million people. Imagine!" Rev. Baul's voice vibrated with the exciting details while Mrs. Baul drew her conclusions as to the impending disaster.

"But I've heard there are no planned neighborhoods, no planned parks and no planned pollution control, and what about all the terrorists?"

This topped them all. For nearly twenty years each new move provided its own adventure, but fear stemming from her childhood still tugged at her heart. One summer the entire family had the privilege of accompanying Rev. Baul to see the land of the Pharaohs. Mind you, it was not to be thought of as vacation. It was strictly a business trip with the family in tow.

Mrs. Baul's stomach had churned on that Egyptian safari, in spite of the thrill of gazing up at the ancient pyramids and floating on a felucca down the Nile. If it hadn't been for all the concrete, the hair-dryer heat, the choking smog, and the imagined lurking terror, the city had potential; it certainly had been something in its day.

Moving to the Middle East at the height of the war on terror seemed insanity itself, especially with the children. To Mrs. Baul this assignment was all the confirmation she needed that Rev. Baul was indeed working with what she came to call a "double opportunity." Her negative observations and growing apprehension would be controlled by silence. This was clearly her husband's next dream assignment.

Two months after "the announcement," as she recalled naming it, they were kissing their goodbyes. Even the beloved family dog was left behind; too harsh an environment for such a pampered soul, and probably too dangerous, Mrs. Baul would add confidentially to her closest group of friends. Try as she might, Mrs. Baul's set smile and determination to make this post one of influence, spiritually speaking, was not enough to keep the voice of God from becoming harder to hear as the city adventure progressed. She had unknowingly set herself up with a fearful outlook. The expression "land of terror" was thrown around at her women's coffees, but never in the presence of her husband.

Of course there were the high points: good vegetarian food, warm weather, and an able staff to manage. She did appreciate the call to prayer, during daylight hours, gracefully echoing from minarets. Undoubtedly these aspects would help ease the longing for an opportunity to revel in nature. So far as she could see, this sort of a city situation was a man-made affair, not at all the way God created this world. However she would make the best of it—throw herself into charity work full-force and keep those distrustful premonitions at bay.

"*Salaam wa'alaykum*, Musa," Grandpa Baul called out in greeting as he and the children started to climb into the sailing felucca floating on the river's edge.

Musa had clearly been sleeping but was never surprised to see them appear, day or night.

"*Wa'alaykum salaam*," answered Musa in welcome. "How was school today, guys?"

"You know, the usual," muttered Joe.

"Yeah, I didn't have much homework so Grandpa said we could come hang out for a while," added Miriam.

"Great! I'm sure ready for some company. Cold soda anyone?"

"Thanks, Musa. You spoil us," smiled Miriam.

"With your grandpa around too you guys will hardly have a chance in life," he joked.

Grandpa Baul was extremely fortunate to have Musa as his captain. He was a highly trained engineer from Sudan who had escaped with his life up the Nile when politics turned sour and the killings began. A severely tall thin man with a broad warm smile, Musa was from what was called a "mixed marriage" (Muslim/Christian parents) and had been granted refugee status in Egypt. Unfortunately that didn't mean he could find a job to match his skills. When he turned up at church with another Dinka friend one day, Grandpa Baul's search for a talented assistant ended.

Getting the boat in working order had taken a patient methodical year. With the help of Miriam's contacts in the "green" world they were able to secure a hollowed out cedar mast from Lebanon and he and Joe had filled it with high tech equipment. At this point the sail was still simply a church advertisement, in honor of Rev. Baul's commission. Computer headquarters lay beneath the boards of the bow and Musa had installed the suitable camouflage coverings.

They had even invited Mrs. Baul to embark for a sunset sail with her husband on one occasion. She had not been eager to set foot into what she imagined to be primitive sailing conditions. However, after rave reviews from their distinguished friends, Sir Peter and Lady Sarah Radcliffe, who had joined Musa on an extended Nile voyage, she conceded to give it a try. Her surprise at the comfortable quarters Musa had made for himself was evident and she thoroughly enjoyed the float despite a mild bout of seasickness. Rev. Baul had unmistakably funded the extravagant setup. Not from his earnings as a priest, of course. It was the generous gift of an artist friend received long before international recognition had confirmed his talent. Rev. Baul did have a natural eye for fine art, yet never did he think his modest collection would soar to such value.

Clearly, Nile River sailing had become a time consuming passion for their children. This was unquestionably Grandpa Baul's influence once again. Mrs. Baul could hardly blame him knowing his childhood reminisces of maneuvering up and down the coastal waters of Maine. Her only concern was safety and he never seemed to question her observations when security priorities lagged.

It was good for the children to get away from electronic screens as often as possible these days. She had heard of too many childhoods disrupted with a variety of inappropriate activities, stories she hadn't wanted to pass on in Rev. Baul's direction. No sense upsetting his equilibrium unnecessarily. Better to expect the best out of their own offspring. And of course she hoped all the community service opportunities she engaged them in would bear fruit as well one day.

The first order of the afternoon's felucca visit was to get Miriam to try out the *hijaab*. Musa already had it secured on board. An extraordinary young linguist, Miriam had a good command of half a dozen languages. However, some tribal dialects, such as the Sinai Bedouin's, were still beyond her without text at hand for deciphering. The Baul trio's research activities were increasingly taking them into uncharted waters, so this latest gadget-in-the-making was an attempt to give her some assistance. Not only would the device permit her into places she wanted to go, but also, the languages she was listening to would be relayed to her by simultaneous translation. She would not get every word, but enough to give her the understanding of what was at hand.

"Musa, have you heard anything about this missing bishop business in Libya?" Grandpa Baul inquired.

"Yes, I got a message this morning from a Berber friend in the Siwa Oasis near the border. He is the day manager of an ecolodge there. At this point they think it may be some sort of a political statement. No one is giving away secrets yet," Musa explained.

"Okay, keep us posted. Mrs. Baul may be asserting her investigative powers so we may have some work ahead of us," Grandpa Baul warned.

"Poor Mom," groaned Miriam. "She really is good hearted. Won't Dad get briefed by the bishop today?"

"I'm already on it. Four-thirty today they have a meeting downtown at the cathedral," Joe read off his screen. "Looks like Bishop Kareem set it up, not Dad. I guess he's okay if he's sending out emails."

"Actually your dad said Bishop Kareem dictates his messages and his assistant writes them up so we can't be certain yet. But I think we need to tune in and see if there are any ways we can help out. I know my son is too proud to come asking," exclaimed Grandpa. "By the way, your mother's panic this morning about the new *muezzin* turned out just as your dad suspected. Modern new speakers installed with prerecorded prayer calls thrown in as a bonus."

"Dear Mrs. Baul," chirped in Musa. "Believe it or not she's braver than when I first met her. Remember what she thought of me when she found the receipt for some of the felucca equipment costs?"

Shaking heads concluded the discussion. Actually, Grandpa Baul had received the brunt of that accusation. His daughter-in-law was convinced he was swindling money from his own son, for the total of the "invisible" electronic supplies were presented as disguised purchases.

"Can I try out this headscarf first?" asked Miriam.

"Musa, can you get her wired? Joe you get us on standby at the meeting while I put in this language CD. Wretched time I had securing it from the librarian at the American University," Grandpa complained. "Little tolerance for imaginative rule bending these days, but she flexed in the end."

"Where did this material come from, Musa?" Miriam asked.

"A Gebeleya sheikh in the Sinai. They're the only tribe in the region that doesn't originate from the Arab peninsula—they're of Macedonian descent. Emperor Justinian sent them to serve and protect St. Catherine's Monastery back in the 6th century," Musa elaborated.

"Are they Christian?" asked Miriam.

"No, but they didn't convert to Islam until the early 1800s," Musa clarified. "Hey, Moses is my namesake you know. I love that part of the country."

"Stand still Miriam," Grandpa called from the front of the boat. "Let's give this thing a try."

"Ouch. It's screeching!" shouted Miriam.

"Drat. Can you give me a hand here, Joe?" asked Grandpa.

"Coming," Joe answered. "We're on the air downtown in five."

"Okay. Wait. Something is coming through now," Miriam said eagerly. She listened intently for a minute or more. "It sounds Berber, maybe even Siwi?"

"Good girl, Miriam. You've got it," Grandpa cheered. "Musa, how about putting some kind of thin flexible camel leather inside to hold things more securely?"

"I'll look into that. I can get down to the Khan el-Khalili tomorrow for some shopping," Musa suggested. "I don't know what I'll attach it with but I'll figure it out."

Before the Baul trio returned home they watched Musa's experienced hands as he took two of Rev. Baul's Egyptian Swifts from a waiting cage and tossed them into the air.

"It's Cinnamon and Sugar!" realized Miriam.

"None other," answered Musa. "You named them well. They don't seem to like to be separated." Musa's work with Rev. Baul's young racers had become a daily ritual. The birds were sure to beat them back home.

"Bishop Kareem," exclaimed Rev. Baul. "It's so good to see you. I was worried when I read the newspaper this morning. What is going on?"

"Thank you for coming downtown," Bishop Kareem replied in his reserved yet friendly manner. "I'm overwhelmed with calls from the press. The government wants an official statement, not to mention a long list of international new agencies, and I have no idea what's going on. How is your lovely wife, and family, by the way?" Even under dire stress the bishop would not forget to ask after Mrs. Baul. Her numerous charitable efforts had won his favor and he had presented her the honored Seal of the Diocese award last year.

"All are fine, thank you, and yours?" the bishop nodded politely in response. "I thought the reopening of St. Mary's in Tripoli was going smoothly," said Rev. Baul as he stared down at his boss's disheveled thinning hair. "Does Lambeth Palace know which bishop Libya is talking about?"

"They are the ones calling me. The Archbishop of Canterbury's secretary has left two messages. I'm still waiting for reports from passport entry to see if they can at least give *me* a name. It's embarrassing this whole business," moaned the bishop. "I need to get answers and quickly. Actually I was hoping that your friend Kubri may have an unofficial connection that could sort this out sooner."

"Sure. I'm glad you got to meet him the other day. You were the first bishop he's ever met," explained Rev. Baul. "I'm not sure I know him well enough yet to probe into that realm but I'll see what I can do."

"Well at least we know Bishop Kareem is safe," exclaimed Grandpa Baul.

"I can't imagine Kubri knows anything," mused Miriam. "But he may have more connections than we think. Maybe we need to have Mom host a dinner party and get him invited."

"Yeah, it's about time we have another try with the *sheesha* water pipe," said Joe excitedly. "Mom will ban them to the garden after dinner for sure. That mouthpiece was a major failure. Have you had time to try doing something with the hose, Grandpa?"

"Yes, but I don't think it's perfected by any means," Grandpa replied. "At least in the garden we have back-up options."

"Musa, do you know anything about Kubri?" asked Grandpa Baul.

"Probably not much more than Rev. Baul has told you," answered Musa. "He is very proud of his direct descent from the Prophet Muhammed, as he should be. Didn't he spend some time in America recently?"

"No, Dad complained that his visa request had been denied," explained Miriam. "Being a famous artist over here doesn't guarantee open doors there I guess."

"I'm sure any background research would have pulled up the fact his father, a Tarabin Bedouin chief, was outspoken on the subject of Gaza," pointed out Musa. "That wouldn't help his case any these days."

"Miriam, see if you can get Mom to think it was her idea," suggested Joe.

-4-

Donkey Rescue

Kubri and Rev. Baul shared an agreeable visit that afternoon. Kubri was indeed a talker and never short of opinions or laughter. Rev. Baul made no secret of the enjoyment he experienced in the presence of his friend's twinkling brown eyes, his dark twitching moustache and a demeanor that suited his short stocky build. As their *sheeshas* bubbled happily, Rev. Baul stepped into the age-old discussion of friends and family connections. Who you knew in this part of the world was crucial.

"Kubri, you're well established here in Cairo," Rev. Baul affirmed. "Do you have any high-up connections in the government or national security world?"

"Well, visibly, I guess not. It's a pretty well known fact though, that my cousin is with the secret police," he added proudly. "He has been decorated, privately of course, on more than one occasion."

"Is there any way you can try to find out the identity of the missing bishop?" asked Rev. Baul.

"For you my friend, I will find out the name of this mystery bishop."

At dinner that evening Rev. Baul mentioned his time with Kubri in the course of conversation, omitting his connections with the secret police for now.

"He is warm and transparent, truly the most fully alive Arab I've ever met," pronounced Rev. Baul admiringly. "I would love for him to meet you all sometime."

"Well why not invite him over for a meal soon?" Mrs. Baul jumped on the idea before realizing the apprehension overtaking her once again. She didn't dare ask if this Kubri was bearded. How humiliating her unfounded prejudices would appear. Who could be afraid of beards and headscarves?

"What a wonderful idea," her husband affirmed. "Thank you, my love."

Grandpa Baul wondered at her verbal eagerness. The chance to host Kubri would serve their purposes as well. He was certain that *sheesha* smoking would be an essential part of hospitality if Rev. Baul's description of "the most fully alive Arab I've ever met," proved to be true.

Part way through dinner, Mrs. Baul rehashed the morning's off tune call to prayer incident before delicately broaching the subject of the missing bishop.

"Darling, I was at book club this morning and Madame Napoleon told us all about a new mystery, a missing or possibly kidnapped bishop of some sort," Mrs. Baul innocently queried. Her friend would of course have her political channels feeding her news and Mrs. Baul was clearly hoping for something of her own to report back.

"Yes, in fact it's all over the news and I met with Bishop Kareem today to discuss it," her husband generously shared his version, leaving out the Kubri inquiry of course.

"Really?" asked Mrs. Baul surprised she had not heard anything sooner in the day.

"At first I was worried Bishop Kareem's safety was in jeopardy but thankfully that wasn't the case," he explained.

"Madame Napoleon said something about Libya and a Banana Bishop?" she probed further.

"Banana Bishop?" he asked. "You don't mean that guy we met in Tunisia way back?"

"I have no idea really," noted Mrs. Baul. "Seemed very farfetched to me."

"I agree. That sounds like premature speculation and most assuredly rumor based," Rev. Baul concluded.

"Excuse me, Rev. Baul," one of the household staff discretely entered the dining room interrupting dessert.

"Yes Shaban, please do come in," Rev. Baul said warmly.

"There is a telephone call for you," he continued. "Would you like to speak to the Donkey Rescue president or should a message be taken?"

"Thank you very much," he replied. "I will take it if you all don't mind me deserting the grand finale of this wonderful meal."

"We need to get started on our homework," Miriam announced with a glance toward her brother.

"Yeah, I have a math test tomorrow," Joe excused himself politely.

Rev. Baul retired to the shelter of his home office as the family immediately dispersed.

"Miriam, stay with your mom," mouthed Grandpa as he signaled for Joe to follow him.

Miriam nodded and pursued Mrs. Baul who was scurrying toward her bedroom, conveniently located on the ground floor, adjoining Rev. Baul's office. Grandpa and

Joe darted into the computer room on the other side and took up their usual post. One button later and the office appeared on their screen. Grandpa Baul was proud of his work and Joe indulged him with likeminded enthusiasm. If the phone call were indeed sensitive then it would be crucial to distract Mrs. Baul. Miriam knew how to work tactical strategy with her mother better than anyone. She knew Grandpa and Joe would give her the details when they debriefed later.

"Miriam, dear," Mrs. Baul said nonchalantly when discovered with her ear against the wall. "Do you know anything about this Donkey Rescue business?" she asked, shamelessly trying to cover her tracks. "Madame Napoleon was telling me today that she would like to donate to its cause through the charity fundraising program this year."

"I don't know Mom," replied Miriam. "That's cool that someone is helping the donkeys here though. I hate it when I see them hobbling along overloaded."

"Yes, I do too dear," added her mother.

"They seem so much happier in Luxor and Aswan, away from the big city setting," observed Miriam. "Why don't you just ask Dad about the donkey thing? Aren't you usually the one people talk to about charity stuff?"

"Well, I think I will once we have a chance to unwind from the demanding day," Mrs. Baul coughed tactfully. "How was school today?"

"Fine."

"Was it my turn to pick you up?" asked Mrs. Baul apprehensively.

"No, Grandpa picked us up."

"Good. I figured you'd call if I'd forgotten. I had to bring cookies to cheer someone up this afternoon as well as a coffee meeting so I hoped I hadn't miscalculated things. Did you come straight home?"

"I had a great day, Mom," said Miriam ignoring the probing questions. "I better go finish up my homework before it gets too late."

"Okay sweetheart. See you later," said Mrs. Baul as she kissed her daughter's pretty brunette head and sent her on her way. As Miriam had guessed, when her mother again put her ear to the wall, she found the telephone call had ended.

Miriam made her way through the back garden to Grandpa Baul's workshop impatient to begin their debriefing rendezvous.

"Hey sis," Joe's voice made her jump when he finally appeared.

"Any details out of inspector Mom?"

"Oh yeah, she's got suicide donkey bombers planning to assassinate presidents!" Miriam answered sarcastically.

Grandpa chuckled. "Not a thing out of the ordinary in your dad's telephone conversation. The Donkey Rescue guy had to cancel his meeting this morning so they've rescheduled for tomorrow at 10am."

"But we'll be at school," pointed out Miriam.

"Yes I know. I'll cover it just in case, but I think your mom is chasing down ghost caravans again," guessed Grandpa.

"You're probably right. We only have two more days of school this week and then a four day weekend," Miriam announced.

"Oh I forgot!" Joe cheered.

"Good timing," said Grandpa. "I'm sure by then things will be getting hotter, at least with the missing bishop rumor. The press isn't letting up on that one."

Mrs. Baul appeared from her bedroom quite flushed and sauntered off into the kitchen to secure an after dinner drink for her husband. Before retiring for the night she double-checked all the door locks and confirmed that the night guard was at his post. Later, as she handed her husband a pair of misplaced reading glasses he was aimlessly searching for, she subtly posed a few curious questions.

"Any interesting news?" queried Mrs. Baul in reference to her husband's telephone call.

"Oh no, not at all. Just the Donkey Rescue man," explained Rev. Baul.

His vague and stumbling response confirmed her suspicions; she was on the track toward something big. She still could not link the simultaneous happenings of the bishop's disappearance and the Donkey Rescue business, but she would in time. Perhaps Madame Napoleon had turned up something important at her dinner party.

Intuition was now hinting that Rev. Baul's friend Kubri, whom he'd mentioned so often recently, was possibly tied up in the center of this intrigue. She must push through the anxiety gnawing inside and talk to her staff about arranging the dinner party. If she could establish a link with this Kubri as well then she might be able to blow the top off this whole thing. Of course it would need to be done discretely and professionally, as she didn't want her bent toward exposing truth to overshadow Rev. Baul's crucial influence in the region. Also there was the extreme danger to consider. But best to work toward preventing a crisis rather than having to face one head on.

Before bed Rev. Baul retired briefly to the garden to visit his elaborate pigeon loft. He often commented that his favorite form of relaxation was sitting on the bench outside and listening to his pigeons cooing. Even Mrs. Baul enjoyed the excitement of watching his athletic pigeons race, yet she knew his true satisfaction came from pondering their creation and the rare markings of their breeding. The brown and khaki barless birds were his latest pride and joy, but he wasn't a purest by any means. He was adamantly outspoken against the practice of culling his flock and he fed wild pigeons, like his feathered friend *Farrouk,* as willingly as his expensive domesticated ones.

Their garden provided a safe shelter for a variety of birds. Even the ground feeding Hoopoes had built nests in the yard and could be seen daily, digging with their dark long beaks in the grass and fanning their black spotted orange crests at the sound of any intruders in their territory.

"Hello, son," said Grandpa Baul as he stepped into the garden.

"Hi Dad," he replied, startled at first. "Isn't the night perfect?"

"Yes, it's beautiful," agreed Grandpa as he joined him on the observation bench. "How are your pigeons? Are you doing okay, son?"

"I'm fine. Thanks for asking," responded Rev. Baul. "Just musing about my Pentecost sermon for next week."

"I heard you mention a Donkey Rescue charity," probed Grandpa.

"Yes. It sounds like a fine organization. They take in sick donkeys but also educate families on how to take care of them so they'll live longer and enhance their own livelihoods. The local man who runs it has been a veterinarian for over twenty years and has even designed some affordable harnesses that are much more humane than the makeshift ones," Rev. Baul had clearly found a kindred spirit.

"I'm glad to hear that," said Grandpa before changing the subject. "Musa was mentioning something about a pigeon race in the Siwa Oasis over the long weekend. Have you heard anything about it?"

"No, I haven't. Unfortunately I haven't been able to sit in the pigeon cafes these last few weeks. I've been too busy doing things the bishop needs an extra hand with," explained Rev. Baul.

"You have been more busy than usual."

"The race sure sounds like an adventure though," added his son. "I know my lovely wife would enjoy a respite from the city again soon. Just have to downplay things so she doesn't think I'm getting obsessed with the pigeons again."

"She blamed that theory on me, not you," his father responded. "I guess the fact we weren't able to accommodate your dream of raising pigeons as a child really has me looking like the bad guy."

"Yes, and I'm still overcompensating and making up for lost time I guess."

Rev. Baul often joined his father and Musa for an evening gathering at the neighborhood pigeon fanciers' café. Discussions of issues concerning the sport of pigeon flying could stretch long into the night. Accomplished show bird or flying judges frequently reiterated standards that had been passed on verbally for many generations. Differences among beginners often needed settling, and betting was a standard part of the system in Egypt.

They had learned a lot about their own Egyptian Swifts, developed over many years of selective breeding in the region, but all descendants from the Rock Pigeon, *Columba livia*. They were known for their long wings and tails and their comparatively short beaks. However one usually had to choose between breeding for show or for racing. The ultimate goal for a flying bird was to reach a combination of the two but Rev. Baul's loft currently had its sights set on speed and endurance.

"I'll see if Musa knows any more details," suggested Grandpa. "Those couple one year olds have probably had enough training to try a long trek. I know Musa has increased their distances regularly and they've performed well on solo flights."

"True," nodded Rev. Baul. "I'd be curious to see how they do on a track they've never seen before. Siwa is over 300 miles away I would think."

"Yes, Musa said 350 miles," Grandpa confirmed. "Less than ten hours of flying time I would guess. The Oasis is only 30 miles from the Libyan border."

"Interesting. Actually I'm meeting Musa at dawn tomorrow to add another mile onto the route of those racers," added Rev. Baul.

-5-

The threat

Monday morning brought forth a flurry of activity from the Baul's home telephone. Rev. Baul was still doing pigeon business with Musa and the kids were already off at school; Grandpa Baul had finished his morning run and heard the monitoring system in his workshop beeping urgently as he stepped out of the shower. He had planned to screen his son's meeting with the Donkey Rescue this morning but he guessed Mrs. Baul was now busy putting her own plans into place before she headed off for her weekly visit to the children's cancer hospital. No question she would take priority in his day's tasks. Oh for the day when he could putter around his creative headquarters and perfect his inventions.

"Madame Napoleon, please. Is that you? Good morning," said Mrs. Baul

"Hello dear friend," replied Madame. "I'm so glad you called. We must meet as soon as possible. I have much to report from the reception last night."

"Wonderful! How about 10 o'clock at our corner table?" suggested Mrs. Baul.

"Perfect. I'll be there. Cheers," she said in her flawless British accent.

"Okay. See you then," Mrs. Baul answered as she hung up briefly and placed another call.

"Yes, a listing for Donkey Rescue in Cairo, please," requested Mrs. Baul.

"What region of Cairo, Madame?" was the response.

"Oh dear. Try Giza, Zamalek, Garden City, Maadi, please search the whole city if you can," she implored.

Minutes later the operator concluded, "No such listing, Madame."

"For certain?" asked Mrs. Baul.

"Not by that name. I can only go by what you tell me," the operator explained.

"Thank you for trying. Goodbye," she answered courteously.

Momentarily discouraged, Mrs. Baul descended upon her kitchen staff and engaged their support for the Kubri dinner gathering to be set for the following evening. She would confirm numbers and finalize the menu later but intended it to be an intimate setting, perhaps merely Kubri and his wife, if he were married. It would be too short notice to include the EU Ambassador and Madame Napoleon. Another time.

Minutes later Mrs. Baul's telephone was ringing again. Grandpa tuned in just in case.

"Hello, Baul residence," Mrs. Baul answered.

"Is this Mrs. Baul?" came a deep muffled voice.

"Why yes it is, who is this?"

"I cannot say but if you want more information on the donkey business you must do as I say,"

"What? Why are you calling me?" asked Mrs. Baul her pulse now racing.

"You must agree not to tell Madame Napoleon about this or her life will be endangered."

"Goodness, I must hang up now if you're going to threaten harm," stated Mrs. Baul as bravely as she could muster.

"You will find a message in the small pyramid chamber between the Sphinx and the Great Pyramid at Giza."

"What?" gasped Mrs. Baul. "This is ridiculous. I demand to know who is calling."

The line went dead. She stood in a state of shock for a moment, wondering what to do next. Dark visions swirled around in her mind, forcing her to sit down and compose herself. It seemed impossible to face such a scenario without the wise advice of her friend. After a few calming minutes she took a deep breath, gathered herself together and headed to her bedroom to organize her purse for the day.

The door to Rev. Baul's study was cracked open slightly as Mrs. Baul passed by still feeling disoriented and shaken. She paused and peered in silently, did not find her husband present, and eased the door open, just enough to squeeze her ample figure through. It seemed an opportune moment not to be missed. Without gloves on hand this would have to be a superficial perusal.

Immediately a brightly colored brochure on the corner of Rev. Baul's desk caught her eye: Kubri's art studio downtown Zamalek. Of course! Madame Napoleon would see the necessity of such a visit today. Most likely her driver would already know of the gallery. Mrs. Baul committed the address to memory, glanced around with alacrity, and slipped out noiselessly.

Back in the cover of her bedroom, Mrs. Baul carefully filled her purse. Strangely her cell phone battery had depleted again sooner than usual. She must remember to ask Joseph about that. She opened up the secret compartment in her jewelry box on the dresser guardedly and pulled out her set of lock pick tools, sunglasses that worked like a rear-view mirror, lockout drops and a small can of clue spray. One could never be too certain what a day may bring forth, especially with the recent sinister sounding phone call. They certainly were dealing with experts this time, all the more confirmation they were on the trail of something significant.

"Darling! Can I order you the usual?" Madame Napoleon floated around the corner to find Mrs. Baul holding their table.

"Yes. Thank you. I need all the caffeine I can get this morning," Mrs. Baul smiled.

Within minutes their conference was online. Months ago Grandpa Baul and the children had placed a listening device underneath this notorious table. They had tried to install a roving bug feature in Mrs. Baul's cell phone but for some reason it was not reliable if her phone was switched off. Last year when she started getting suspicious of everything and everyone, she started turning off her phone at her clandestine meetings and began to secure reconnaissance items of her own. Although in her hands they were more likely acquired for show and psychological satisfaction, Grandpa Baul never wanted to leave such plotting sessions to guesswork. He was extremely curious to see if his daughter-in-law would spill the news of the telephone threat. The mysterious voice had not remained on the line long enough to secure a valid trace.

"New developments. I'm sure of it," Madame Napoleon leaned over the table in eager anticipation.

"About the Donkey Rescue business or the kidnapped bishop?" asked Mrs. Baul.

"Both," replied Madame.

"I knew it. There had to be a connection," she beamed proudly.

"I don't have proof. Just inklings," Madame Napoleon said eagerly. "Remember the nuclear power station up on the Mediterranean coast? It was abandoned about twenty years ago but it still maintains a small experimental nuclear reactor. I am certain Egypt has done atomic research, but full disclosure to the UN's watchdog has been shady."

"What do you mean by 'shady'?" probed Mrs. Baul.

"Well according to my sources there was some sort of misunderstanding over exactly what had to be disclosed."

"But I thought the government had signed a treaty to say they would only develop nuclear energy peacefully?" Mrs. Baul inquired.

"Well, you know how documents can be worded with loopholes and all. Yes, they've agreed to international supervision but there's been no action on any front for years," she clarified. "Until now."

"What?" asked Mrs. Baul.

"An announcement has been made that a nuclear power station will be constructed at El-Dabaa up on the coast," Madame Napoleon explained. "Doesn't the timing of this seem suspicious to you?"

"It sure does. That can't be very far from Libya," Mrs. Baul deliberated. "But how would the Donkey Rescue fit in with that? Or the kidnapped bishop for that matter?"

"I don't know yet, but we are on the trail of something big, very big," gleamed Madame Napoleon. "When I tried to probe my husband for information last night before bed he flew into a frenzy. I know we are on the right track this time."

"Yes, we've stumbled on something of an incredibly large scale to be sure," Mrs. Baul nodded in agreement. "I just wish I didn't feel so nervous about it all. Some days I wonder if my imagination just works overtime. Has our shipment arrived yet?"

"I completely forgot in all the excitement," Madame Napoleon explained as she reached for her purse. "Don't worry; I'm a bit edgy myself. The diplomatic pouch arrived yesterday. Did I tell you the stun pens were out of stock, but the pepper spray rings and the UV pens made it? I don't know how we're going to get away with wearing the rings though. If you ask me, the plastic jewels set on top can be seen from across the room."

"Oh, they are quite horrible," Mrs. Baul agreed as she scrutinized them. "Not something either of us would be flashing around on our fingers. We could put them on our key chains just to have at the ready."

"That's an excellent suggestion," settled Madame Napoleon as she glanced at her watch and they both rose to leave. Just outside the café a rush of children encircled Mrs. Baul with large smiles and out held hands, waiting eagerly for the candy they knew she carried for them in her purse. The women continued their conversation along insignificant themes for a while until both agreed that a trip to investigate Kubri's art gallery was called for after their visit to the cancer hospital. Only a slight bit of creative discretion would be needed to disguise them from recognition upon a second meeting.

"Musa. Good morning. I need your help," Grandpa Baul explained through a fuzzy sounding cell phone. "Let me call you back on my secure landline." He had tried to text message the kids but lunch break was still an hour off and in reality they couldn't do anything before school got out anyway.

"Hi there. We have a problem," said Grandpa Baul.

"Mrs. Baul?" Musa asked.

"Flawless intuition, Musa. She, and you know who, are out to save the world again," he laughed nervously. "You'd think the fear factor would shut them down not spur them on. We have our work cut out for us."

"What can I do?" inquired Musa.

"See what you can find out about the nuclear plant in El-Dabaa up on the coast," requested Grandpa. "Also, she got a threatening phone call that sounded very much like a prank to me but can you double check that the Donkey Rescue charity is a valid organization?"

"Will do."

"Is there anything new from Siwa on the bishop?"

"The latest is that this is all a hoax," Musa reported. "There are a couple missing jeeps in a caravan fleet but that isn't seen as very unusual, considering the hassle of police paper work before heading out to explore the sand sea. Could just be that a few guides wanted to practice their sand boarding or have a quiet picnic out on the dunes. It's low season for tourists."

"Anything from the lodges?" asked Grandpa.

"I'm still working a few bribes for that one. My friend actually works at one but there seem to be some legal implications preventing answers to our questions. We're standing in a long line right now," Musa explained.

"Okay. Keep me posted. What do you know about Kubri's art studio downtown? Is that an above board affair?" Grandpa Baul queried.

"Man, I'm telling you that guy is as clean as they come. His name says it all. *Kubri* is Arabic for *bridge*, you know. He's building them, not blowing them up. Mrs. Baul's idea, right?" asked Musa.

"How did you guess?" laughed Grandpa.

"I'll see if someone downtown knows anything more. You never know if someone is playing him that he isn't aware of himself, connections being what they are sometimes," replied Musa.

"Thank you, Musa," said Grandpa. "I'm going to head downtown on the Metro myself and see what these ladies come up with. All pretty innocent at this stage but I didn't like the tone of their voices this morning. Much too eager for something of grand proportions, I'm afraid. Also, I need to get some *sheesha* tobacco and a pot of tea brewing for Kubri's visit tomorrow night."

"I'll get going on this research and let you know if I find anything significant," said Musa. "You'll want the usual tobacco, right?"

"Yes. I've got the half dozen herbs I need brewing in my lab for the tea. It won't hurt to try a double tactic this time," Grandpa explained.

"Okay. I'll get the tobacco ready, going to give it a mango flavored twist this time. Good luck with the ladies!" cheered Musa.

"Oh!" startled Mrs. Baul. "Look, that painting!"

What began as a nonchalant entry of two blond haired women with hats and sunglasses into the art gallery had just attracted the attention of the artist in residence. Fortunately for the ladies, Kubri was nowhere to be found, which served to relax the guarded demeanor of Mrs. Baul and her astute companion.

"Well now," observed Madame Napoleon. "What a well cared for donkey. An excellent capturing of his persevering spirit."

"But look, in the background. The Shali ruins in the Siwa Oasis, right?" inquired Mrs. Baul as she adjusted her hairdo ever so slightly.

"Yes, I think you're correct, although I've only seen them in tour books," she said. "The ruins certainly do look like muddy salt blocks soaked to the ground by unexpected rain. Could anything else explain that?"

"What kind of a coincidence could this be?" asked Mrs. Baul. "I am convinced there is more to this painting than meets the eye."

The artist had cleaned her hands upon hearing the women enter and came over to answer any questions.

"Welcome to the gallery," said the artist.

"Thank you very much," Mrs. Baul answered politely.

"Is this your first visit?"

"Yes it is in fact," Madame Napoleon added.

"Did the famous artist Kubri paint this donkey scene?" queried Mrs. Baul.

"He crafted this masterpiece himself and that is the Shali ruins in the background," she confirmed. "Most of what you see displayed here is his unless marked as one of his students."

One thing led to another until Mrs. Baul spontaneously declared she wanted to purchase the art piece, "for further exploration" she murmured to her friend. She handed the woman her credit card and pondered the excitement of the latest development. Madame Napoleon enthusiastically agreed to bring the painting to her garden's guesthouse quarters for a closer inspection. No one would suspect them there. She had designated one of the rooms for her exclusive use only. Lights and equipment were already in place. Mrs. Baul wondered if her "x-ray spray" might be able to detect something through the backside of the canvas. That is if there was indeed some type of code or message involved with this innocent looking work of art; indeed a very clever guise it would be.

Grandpa Baul stood by helplessly, awkwardly disguised as an old Arab tea peddler on the corner outside the gallery. His impromptu plans had not given him the proximity he had hoped for. Eventually his daughter-in-law emerged, virtually dancing on air, and leading the way for the loading of her massive acquisition into the waiting vehicle. He shook his head in disbelief and wondered what would be his son's reaction. The painting was completely wrapped, but it was certain to be unveiled at dinner that evening with great drama and hoopla.

-6-

The Rt. Rev. Edwin Cornwall-McGrath III

Rev. Baul's meeting with the Donkey Rescue had taken place downtown Cairo near the cathedral. Very sound organization indeed. Kubri had left a message on his cell phone inviting him to lunch at their usual café. Rev. Baul would have just enough time before attending to a parishioner back at church. He could possibly postpone that a bit if necessary.

"Hello, my friend," called Kubri as he saw Rev. Baul step out of a black and white taxi.

"Kubri, good to see you," replied Rev. Baul warmly.

The day was pleasant and Rev. Baul was delighted to join him at a sidewalk table. The center of city action refreshed his spirits: cars honking, shoppers walking by and his favorite *taameya* sandwich for lunch. Food was ordered round and drinks arrived promptly. The hour settled into an enjoyable rhythm. Families were asked about, dinner the following evening offered and accepted, and finally the question of the missing bishop addressed.

"News from my cousin is mysterious," offered Kubri. "No bishop that Security knows of has passed into Libya within the last week."

"Really?" asked Rev. Baul.

"There was a potential red flag at customs on a flight into Cairo from England," he explained. "A British citizen was traveling on a tourist visa that was purchased at the airport. The hotel registration listed on his customs clearance card was of an ecolodge in the Siwa Oasis."

"Which one?" interrupted Rev. Baul.

"I don't know for sure. There are several options on that front and but most owned by the same businessman who confirmed that this gentleman's passport was registered upon arrival but he had not been seen after breakfast his first morning. The owner assumed he had gone out on a tourist trek to the desert for a few days. A waiter at the restaurant reportedly saw a local guide in heated conversation with him, most likely haggling a suitable excursion price."

"Has anyone searched his room?"

"Yes. His suitcase is still there but his backpack and ID are missing," Kubri elaborated.

"Did you get his name?" asked Rev. Baul.

"This is all at least third hand information I'm afraid. My cousin pronounced a name that reminded me of those corned beef sandwiches you like to eat," replied Kubri.

"Not Cornwall-McGrath is it?" Rev. Baul suggested.

"That sounds about right. Yes, it was double-barreled. Some sort of highfaluting British gentry or something?" asked Kubri.

"Something resembling that. He works for the ABC, Archbishop of Canterbury, at Lambeth Palace in London.

I met him in seminary way back. Odd that. I wonder if the archbishop is missing him?" mused Rev. Baul.

"That may be a good place to start," Kubri suggested.

"You're right. Can I fill Bishop Kareem in on this? He'd be so grateful."

"Of course, my friend. It's going to catch the foreign press sooner or later. Just leave my contacts as anonymous. Things will get confirmed officially once word gets out," said Kubri.

"Guaranteed," pronounced Rev. Baul.

"Poor Siwa. They take pride in their quiet undisturbed village. They've been resisting permission for that newly built airport to bring in large commercial flights. Lack of desire to embark on a ten-hour drive from Cairo seems to be protecting them for now."

"Nothing is going to prepare them for the descent of snooping foreigners," cringed Rev. Baul.

"It will be a shock," agreed Kubri.

"Thanks so much for all your help with this."

"You are very welcome! For you my friend, I am at your service."

Once lunch was cleared Rev. Baul headed over to inform the bishop of the latest developments. He waited around to hear the ABC's secretary confirm that the missing bishop had indeed left for a two-week vacation but the secretary assumed it had been to his cottage on the coast of Wales as usual.

"Rev. Baul, I need an official press release generated as soon as possible," explained the overwhelmed Bishop Kareem. "Would you be willing to draft that for me?"

"I suppose I could rearrange my schedule and get a version done for you to approve," he agreed.

"Thank you so much," said Bishop Kareem. "I'll have your English version translated into Arabic as well."

"I'll get right on it," he assured the bishop.

"The other thing I think may be important is to arrange some sort of investigator to head to Siwa that could be the eyes and ears of the Church," stated Bishop Kareem.

"Under the circumstances and seeing that a long holiday weekend is approaching, can I recommend that I go as your discrete representative?" Rev. Baul suggested. "There is a pigeon race from Siwa to Cairo this weekend that I'm eager to be part of."

"A perfect cover," declared the bishop. "Take your family with you. I know your lovely wife could use a break from the pressures of city life."

"Thank you, Bishop Kareem. I will be back in time to deliver my Pentecost sermon on Saturday evening."

"Thank you, Rev. Baul. You are my eyes and ears."

As Musa's Siwan contacts had proven to be slow with results, he determined to take matters one-step further. While shopping at the Khan el-Khalili bazaar he decided to diverge from his list and visit the local pigeon breeders. Some of the top veteran fanciers of the Middle East frequented these parts. There was undeniably a buzz in the air about Saturday's marathon race from Siwa to Cairo.

Musa quickly located Rev. Baul's feather merchant supplier and asked for the race entry details. All looked typical: perch fee, race fee, registered ring prefix details, proof of vaccines and stamped wings for youngsters in case they strayed in the race. Since Musa had had a similar hobby as a young boy in Sudan, Rev. Baul often consulted him on racing strategies. Occasionally on Fridays, Rev. Baul's day off, Musa accompanied the family on visits to the bazaar. Mrs. Baul would wander off to bargain the best price for spices and alabaster, while the rest of them would gather around the bird market.

As far as Musa could surmise, the only way they would be able to get to the bottom of the missing bishop mystery was to establish a ground presence. Armed with the race information and the reverend's eagerness to fly his birds, the weekend could prove very interesting.

Dinner that evening was full of chatter. Rev. Baul freely shared his findings about the missing bishop, since he had written an official press release for the diocese and all. The family listened attentively. He did hold back his own investigations into the matter but only Mrs. Baul seemed in the dark on his sources. Grandpa Baul caught the unmistakable gleam in her eye when the bishop's name was revealed.

"The Rt. Rev. Edwin Cornwall-McGrath III. Imagine! How excessively exciting that we know him personally," Mrs. Baul exclaimed. "I wondered from the start if it might be he. I do of course hope he's all right. You don't think anything untoward has happened to him, do you dear?"

"Oh no darling must just be a mix up of some kind. These things do sort themselves out in time," Rev. Baul assured her. "Siwa is such a quiet oasis."

"Dad, did Musa talk to you about the pigeon race?" asked Joe.

"Indeed he did, son," offered Rev. Baul. "In fact I would like to propose that we take a family leave and do a bit of sightseeing this week."

"Really?" gaped Mrs. Baul.

"To Siwa?" asked Joe.

"Oh Dad, you mean it?" asked Miriam.

"Why not? Musa has explained what a great opportunity this would be to race our two young pigeons and I cannot think of a reason not to," Rev. Baul announced happily.

"You mean Cinnamon and Sugar are ready to race?" asked Miriam excitedly.

"Both Musa and I agree it's time to test them on a long haul," her father confirmed.

"How exciting! I've longed to see the beauty of the desert's rolling waves of desert sand," Mrs. Baul uninhibitedly proclaimed. "What a treat. Thank you, sweetheart." The moment she'd finished her sentence a sense of dread enveloped her. Was it the haunting nightmare that caused her gnawing fear or an actual premonition?

"When do we leave, son?" asked Grandpa.

"I think I'll charter us a flight for Thursday morning. That still gives us a couple days. I've asked Musa to join us as well," stated Rev. Baul. "Are we still on for our weekly lunch date tomorrow, my love?"

"Indeed," smiled Mrs. Baul. "You know I would never turn down such an offer."

As dinner concluded, Grandpa Baul could not help but wonder why they had not all been given the opportunity to rave over Mrs. Baul's new purchase. It did not appear to be an absentminded omission. He was sure Madame Napoleon had not funded the affair, not the way things were loaded into the car with Mrs. Baul at the commanding forefront.

He had missed something in his low-tech reconnaissance mission. It was imperative they finish the adjustments on Mrs. Baul's bracelet tonight. His son had simply asked for the clasp to be fixed, but this proved the exact opportunity the Baul trio needed to install a professional listening device on her person. Coming as a lavish gift from her husband, Mrs. Baul was certain never to be without it in public.

The list of things to do before the Siwa departure was rapidly growing to untold proportions in the mind of Mrs. Baul as she frantically thought through all that needed to be accomplished in the next 48 hours. She would have to see if a friend could fill in for her at the school for deaf children on Thursday. An emergency meeting would need to be arranged at Madame Napoleon's guesthouse quarters for tomorrow. Well, that was planned anyway with the painting investigation awaiting completion. She also needed to decide if she should risk heeding the advice of the threatening telephone caller.

Procedures for the weekend's adventure required methodical thinking, as Madame Napoleon would not be present for brainstorming as events advanced. Goodness. What providence that Kubri would join them for dinner tomorrow evening. Rev. Baul had confirmed he was unmarried, a bit suspicious for this region.

-7-

The painting

"Oh what beautiful artistry!" exclaimed Mrs. Baul when she opened up her husband's generous gift at lunch the following day.

"I worked out the design myself," Rev. Baul explained ardently. "The shells are hand collected, and are only found here in the Red Sea. It is an honor to have such a beautiful wife to dote on."

"Thank you. I am so proud to be your wife," Mrs. Baul replied sincerely before subtly seizing her opportune moment. "My dear, can I ask you a question?"

"Of course. Anything," smiled Rev. Baul, still in an admiring daze.

"What would you do if you were quite sure a close friend of yours was collaborating with criminals unaware?" posed Mrs. Baul as delicately as possible.

"My goodness! I can't imagine ever being in such a position," responded Rev. Baul. "I suppose you should reveal the situation to your friend if you had solid proof."

"What if you didn't have all the pieces linked together but just an inner certainty?" she asked.

"Well, that is a different affair," concluded Rev. Baul. "It could do some unnecessary damage to the relationship if you were shown to be wrong in the end."

Yes, best left unsaid at this point. If Rev. Baul was truly working a double opportunity it could be downright dangerous for him if she uttered her suspicions without enough evidence in hand. Time would lay bare the truth soon enough.

Rev. Baul dropped off his wife at the home of Madame Napoleon after agreeing to stop and buy her friend a large bouquet of sunflowers just in season. She thanked him again for the exquisite gift and promised to be back home in time to supervise the final arrangements for Kubri's dinner party. Mrs. Baul was truly touched by her husband's thoughtfulness and dangled her bracelet in sure view of the observant eyes of her friend.

"Oh, delightful flowers and a new bracelet!" declared Madame Napoleon.

"Thank you. A Red Sea original from my husband just today!" Mrs. Baul explained aglow.

"Surely one of a kind. Very exquisite craftsmanship," she admired. On closer examination the treasured piece of jewelry looked positively ghastly, but no sense in upsetting her goodhearted friend.

"These shells are miracles of creation itself," declared Mrs. Baul. "Anyway, have you unveiled our treasure yet?"

"No, come. Let's get started," she replied.

Curiosity drew the ladies off to their covert quarters. With florescent lights above and a portable ultraviolet light stored on a central table, the work place was well suited for observant analysis. Impatiently they unwrapped the painting and began the search for clues. Madame strongly discouraged her friend from using her "x-ray spray" as the package had made clear its purpose was for the temporary exposure of sealed envelopes. The risk of jeopardizing the expensive canvas was too great. Instead they studied the scene of the painting itself and brooded over the role of Middle Eastern donkeys in everyday life. Established as "beasts of burden," their conclusions necessitated further inspiration.

Before long Mrs. Baul voiced her keen observations.

"Do you see that carrying bag draped over the donkey in the painting?" asked Mrs. Baul.

"Yes, is there some significance to it?"

"Oddly enough it is made of Tunisian basketry materials, not the sturdy hand-woven carpet quality we find here in our own country," Mrs. Baul pointed out. "It is entirely possible that these faithful creatures are being shuttled along the North African coast. Most likely across the Libyan border into Egypt illegally."

"Why on earth would they be doing that?" asked Madame Napoleon not yet following her friend's line of thinking.

"Smuggling," declared Mrs. Baul.

"Smuggling? Smuggling what?"

"There are a number of options along the coastal region that could range from dates to olives to drugs or weapons," explained Mrs. Baul.

So much talk in the media of late produced a simultaneous pronouncement.

"Weapons of mass destruction may be to blame!" exclaimed Madame Napoleon.

"Exactly what came to my mind," her friend confirmed as the repercussions of such a discovery began to take hold. "Obviously it would be too dangerous for the donkeys to carry fully assembled weaponry or biochemical ingredients but crucial individual elements would make sense. These components must be reaching a destination unsuspected by local authorities."

"They must have a headquarters at their disposal so they can assemble things, but where?

"Siwa?" suggested Mrs. Baul.

"El-Dabaa!" realized Madame Napoleon.

"Of course! It all fits together," Mrs. Baul agreed. "All the same, with the kidnapped bishop business on the outskirts of Siwa it may be best to leave nothing to chance."

"I quite agree. Concrete facts are necessary," Madame Napoleon concluded.

Mrs. Baul disclosed her husband's privileged knowledge gathered from Bishop Kareem at the opportune moment. They also discussed the sudden need for Rev. Baul to visit the Siwa Oasis, pigeon race or not. The fact that he had extended the invitation to the whole family was an excellent sign that no one had caught wind of their own maneuverings. If only the danger element wasn't looming so closely. Not for the first time, the thought of hiring a personal bodyguard crossed her mind. Securing a trustworthy guardian would not be easily accomplished so the thought dismissed itself.

"While I'm away in Siwa," Mrs. Baul began, "We must stay in touch through our satellite phones."

"Brilliant idea," affirmed Madame.

In a video game order for Joseph's 13th birthday, Mrs. Baul had disguised a recent credit card expense. The catalog description of a global positioning system service had greatly influenced their purchase. Neither had any experience with such communication devises, but the instruction manual seemed straightforward enough.

"Also, I will do further research through my network of Egyptian connections during the days ahead," announced Madame Napoleon eagerly. "Perhaps a lead will present itself."

"Good thinking. Now is the time for action," Mrs. Baul concluded.

The remaining unresolved topic of discussion was the anticipation of the Kubri dinner visit that evening. Mrs. Baul continued to have very bad vibes about this new friend of Rev. Baul. With what they had just exposed in his painting it seemed vital that they research his background further, if only for the protection of Rev. Baul's reputation. It was agreed that during the serving of after dinner tea, Mrs. Baul would excuse any hovering staff and secure a set of his fingerprints. Madame Napoleon assured her that although she had no personal access to police records, she could file a rush order at the European Union headquarters. She knew just the man for the job.

"I'm home, anyone here?" called Mrs. Baul upon return to the Vicarage.

"Better go intercept her, Miriam," Joe quickly suggested, when their mother's voice reached the vicinity of Grandpa's workshop after school. Even with the white noise machine they ran around the perimeter of their high-tech headquarters to thwart curious ears, they never wanted to run the risk of Mrs. Baul ever setting foot inside. Best if she continued to assume all Grandpa's workshop tinkering was limited to repairing watches, electrical problems, and bird cages. And as in the case of their sailing interests, they figured no further explanation was needed; Mrs. Baul considered it natural for grandchildren to want to be with their grandfather during their free time.

"Okay. I'll be back soon," Miriam said as she darted off to greet her mother.

Grandpa finished bringing Joe up to date on the odd findings from the eavesdropping bracelet earlier that afternoon. Even if he'd witnessed the donkey painting inspection in person, Grandpa was certain the conjectures the women were visualizing were absolutely outrageous.

"How is the serum coming along, Grandpa?" asked Joe.

"Just about perfect," Grandpa observed. "We're lucky your mom likes gardens, and that your dad loves supplying her with rare herbs. I didn't have this valerian last time I brewed up this recipe. It's sometimes used to promote sleep because of the way it interacts with certain brain receptors."

Grandpa proudly ticked off the list: wild lettuce leaf, mistletoe, passionflower, hops flower, chamomile and valerian. If this didn't make an honest truth speaker out of Kubri, nothing would.

"It looks like paste, not tea," said Joe.

"That's the idea for now. Once I get the consistency strength right I'll water it down a bit and deliver it to the kitchen at a timely moment," Grandpa explained.

"Has Musa finished the tobacco yet?" Joe queried.

"Yes, it's on the table there," pointed Grandpa. "See if you can slip that out to the garden with the *sheesha*. If you hide the other flavors your dad will be forced to use this one."

"What all is in it?" asked Joe.

"Same ingredients as this brew, but Musa reconstituted it into mango delight," Grandpa elaborated as he gave full attention to his bubbling concoction. "This stuff is all natural and pretty mild but I don't want to face failure again. We've got to prove to ourselves that Kubri's talk matches his reputation or else we could be dooming ourselves from the start."

"I'll confirm the monitoring system in the fountain is in working order while I'm out there," said Joe grabbing the tobacco as he left Grandpa's workshop.

-8-

Family reconnaissance

"Kubri! *Ahlan wa sahlan*," Rev. Baul exclaimed in welcome when his friend appeared for dinner that evening.

"Hello, friend," he replied as he handed over an enormous bouquet of exotic fresh flowers. "For your wife."

"Thank you! Welcome," Mrs. Baul entered the front hall as soon as she'd heard Kubri arrive. The moment of reckoning was here. "I am so pleased to meet you."

"*Gameelah*, beautiful," responded Kubri, taken back with her beauty. "Please allow me to use my mother tongue in calling you beautiful, *Gameelah*, Madame Baul."

"Why thank you. That's very generous of you," Mrs. Baul responded warmly as she scrutinized him, repeatedly shaking his thick sturdy hands.

Rev. Baul smiled in admiration of his wife and of his friend's generosity. "Very kind of you, Kubri," he stated.

"I only speak the truth," Kubri established with a wide toothed smile.

The evening progressed with great satisfaction. Mrs. Baul put on her bravest face as she probed for mutual charity work connections that might authenticate his character. Grandpa Baul immediately warmed to Kubri's spirit, as did Miriam and Joe, who had anticipated the dinner would be dull. Hardly. Kubri joked and told stories of wild proportions. Laughter mingled with conversation and wonder, as the family shared their meal. When dessert was presented, Rev. Baul announced a toast.

"To my beautiful wife, and the finding of a true heart friend," spoke Rev. Baul with deep sincerity.

"*Shokran*, thank you, I am honored," nodded Kubri.

"Why not join our family this weekend, Kubri?" offered Rev. Baul. "We are going to explore your great Siwa Oasis. A distinguished pigeon race is being celebrated."

"Well, I don't know what to say," Kubri responded. "I've only ever been there once, years ago."

The rest of the entranced Baul family members simply stared with agreeable smiles on their faces. They were all of course taken with this newfound friend, yet wondered as to Rev. Baul's motivations. Was this purely a sightseeing request? Only time would tell. As wooed as she was by this gracious man, Mrs. Baul's conclusions were extremely conflicted.

As expected, Rev. Baul insisted on showing Kubri his much talked about pigeon loft. The creative lighting in the garden served the setting well. Tea was ordered and *sheesha* coals lit. Expressing gratefulness for such an enjoyable evening, Grandpa Baul and the children excused themselves. Mrs. Baul offered to serve the tea herself before retiring for the night.

"Oh, I do apologize," said Mrs. Baul as soon as they'd each taken their small glass Arab teacups. "I see a slight chip on the edge of both of these. How dreadful. Please put them back on the tray. I will exchange them immediately."

"*Gameelah*, stop, we do not mind at all," Kubri responded kindly.

"I do insist," she replied awkwardly.

"Let her Kubri. She won't rest until it's put right," added Rev. Baul. "Thank you darling."

As soon as Mrs. Baul had secured the fingerprints, she made a dash for her bedroom before returning with new glasses. She fumbled momentarily with her bath powder and then carefully pressed clear packaging tape over the remains. Unfortunately in the fluster of procuring the evidence she had completely forgotten which glass belonged to Kubri.

Undeterred she finished her proceedings and sealed them carefully in a plastic bag, clarifying critical instructions with the new pen she'd been given. Prior arrangements had been made for Madame Napoleon's driver to pick up the package first thing the next morning.

As the garden monitoring progressed it became evident to the workshop observers that some additional sleuthing would be necessary. What may have fooled the gentlemen in the garden certainly had not escaped them. Miriam was dispatched for reconnaissance as Joe and Grandpa stayed tuned.

The moment Miriam saw her mother leave her bedroom and head in the direction of the kitchen she slipped into the room to investigate. What she found was not surprising. The "fingerprints" had been discretely laid inside the top section of her mother's jewelry box. She discovered that a blank piece of paper had been inserted into the plastic bag as well. Grandpa had warned her of her mother's new UV pen and she countered the potential problem accordingly. Miriam took out a decoding pen and shined its light onto the paper.

> MN: Sorry mixed up prints.
> Kubri invited to Siwa.
> Go to El-D w/o me.
> Use sat phone only. MB

Miriam committed it to memory and raced back to the workshop. Grandpa and Joe urgently motioned her to silence as she entered. Both men on the screen were just starting to yawn as Kubri introduced the topic of the sale of his most recent painting.

"Yesterday afternoon I hear someone bearing your family name purchased one of my recent landscapes," Kubri explained. "A Siwan scene with a donkey in the foreground, to be exact. You haven't seen that painting yet have you?"

"No, I haven't," replied Rev. Baul honestly. "I don't know anyone else here in Egypt, other than my own family, who bears my family name. Perhaps it was a gift? It wasn't my wife was it?"

"I'm not entirely sure. According to my artist in residence, two blond women came in acting a bit curiously and one declared almost immediately that she must purchase the newly displayed painting. This was no small tourist souvenir," Kubri emphasized.

"How very interesting," pondered Rev. Baul. "It couldn't have been my wife then as she obviously isn't blond. She would definitely have been with her inseparable friend Madame Napoleon for such a venture, but she isn't blond either."

"I could be mistaken, of course," Kubri conceded. "Madame Napoleon, I have heard her name far beyond EU circles. She seems to get more spotlight than her husband these days. Wasn't she wrapped up with that antiquities smuggling scandal recently?"

"My wife assures me the fiasco was rife with rumors, originating with some jealous woman's gossip," defended Rev. Baul. "Madame Napoleon was thwarting the attempt rather than participating in it. She seems awfully well intentioned to be sure. Supports a great number of charities throughout Egypt."

"I have heard that as well," noted Kubri.

"I know my wife has found a kindred spirit across creeds and cultures in her friend."

"Very good to hear," said Kubri as he delicately closed the subject. The timing was certainly not right for enlightening the reverend on the findings of his cousin and the complications surrounding Madame Napoleon's diplomatic immunity.

As soon as Miriam was sure the conversation had ended she burst forth with full disclosure of her recent discovery. At least Grandpa had forestalled the possibility of being thwarted by the new pens. Joe reiterated what Musa had filled them in on that afternoon. He confirmed that El-Dabaa had hit the international papers recently with the announcement of the building of a nuclear power station to generate more energy for the country. The site chosen already had an old reactor in place, yet it needed a complete overhaul as well. But the donkey painting had them all completely stumped. How could weapons of mass destruction emerge from donkey baskets in the minds of these benevolent ladies?

"I'm still frustrated my gallery reconnaissance mission was so sloppy," Grandpa Baul muttered unhappily.

"You did what you could at the time, Grandpa," assured Joe.

"Yeah, and anyway who would have thought something like this could have come out of a simple trip to an art gallery?" added Miriam.

"Still, we must find a more concrete angle," mused Grandpa. "I know in the past, only in the face of impending disaster have we stooped to peer into the often-incriminating pages of your mother's diary. But as plans now seem to inevitably be leading us into Egypt at large, I feel we need to confirm if more than we've heard verbalized is afoot."

"I think you're right, Grandpa," said Miriam.

"So do I," affirmed Joe. "But there's not much more we can do before morning."

"True. I will work on that tomorrow when the coast is clear," agreed Grandpa. "But I'm afraid things have escalated to the point of needing reinforcements."

"What kind of reinforcements?" asked Joe.

"You mean like a backup plan?" asked Miriam.

"Yes, with so many missing pieces floating around we do need to get a backup plan into place. This El-Dabaa accusation could cause real problems. Your mother and her well-intentioned friend are assuming there is a connection between that and the missing bishop."

"You're right," said Miriam. "I know it's unlikely but even so, if any of this was even hinted to the press we could have an international incident on our hands."

"I have no idea how the donkey painting fits into all this," added Grandpa. "Does that make the situation safer or more damaging? I do not know."

"Wow," said Miriam.

"What should we do next?" asked Joe.

When the Baul family had moved to Cairo five years earlier, the first six months of settling in had been an enormous adjustment for Mrs. Baul, as was expected. The school and church had welcomed them warmly but as time passed Mrs. Baul began to exhibit warning signs caused by lingering effects of the harsh environment: her fear of terrorists around every corner for one, lack of nature for her morning walks, and the strain on her compassionate heart in the face of ever-rampant poverty, all began to layer, build and overwhelm her.

Cairo ushered in their first spring with a pounding of the *Khamseen* season, fifty days of sandstorms from the desert. In response to the quality of air, or rather lack of it, Mrs. Baul developed full-blown asthma. The local physician prescribed a list of medicines—inhalers, pills, drops, and syrups—none of which she accepted. Mastering breathing techniques was her determined solution. A long road lay ahead. Rev. Baul had sensed the deteriorating spirits of his brave wife and suggested the only possible solution over dinner one evening.

"I got news from Joseph's godparents today," Rev. Baul ventured. "They are between assignments in England. What would you think about having them come for a visit?"

"What a wonderful idea!" declared Mrs. Baul. "It feels like ages since we've seen them. I would love to have them visit!"

Sir Peter and Lady Sarah Radcliffe. Wouldn't Madame Napoleon be impressed! These two famed physicians had lived all over the world, spoke medical vocabulary in dozens of languages and were fluent in French and Arabic as well. In partnership with North African doctors, the Radcliffes had made heroic progress in raising the standard of medicine throughout the rural Maghreb.

"I will never forget the height of Lady Sarah's career, in my humble opinion—the welcoming of little Joseph into the world safely with her own capable hands," Rev. Baul recounted with great pride and admiration.

"Thirteen years ago now," added Mrs. Baul. "What a memorable occasion!"

Miriam and Joe had to listen to the retelling of their birth stories at every birthday meal celebration they could ever remember. Both kids jumped in with new conversation topics with hopes that they wouldn't have to hear the same old stories yet again.

As dinner progressed, Grandpa Baul was quick to suspect that this well received invitation for the Radcliffes to visit was simply a very costly doctor's house call, for Mrs. Baul was in dire need of a professional evaluation. It wasn't his place to suggest otherwise. Grandpa Baul predicted silently that this proposal would indeed lift his daughter-in-law's spirits. His son had done well again.

Just the thought of a visit from the Radcliffes threw Mrs. Baul into a dedicated cleaning frenzy. Sandstorm season or not she joined her staff in shining windows and readying the property. She rattled off an immediate list of jobs to be done: weeding the herb garden, refilling flower boxes, polishing the silver. A gray cloud may have settled over her head but it would not be proper to allow the likes of Lady Sarah and Sir Peter to be dragged down into such misery. They would of course be certain to spot the telltale signs of depression in her voice and demeanor, but, in a sense, it would be freeing to draw them aside privately. She was confident the Baul family was unaware of her true emotional state.

As the day of the Radcliffe's visit drew near, Mrs. Baul suggested sending an expeditor to meet their flight and whisk them across Cairo. It was not to be heard of, they were in need of adventure. When the steaming Metro car finally delivered these two beloved people into their presence, they greeted each other with great warmth. Sir Peter had the 72-hour visit mapped out to the smallest detail. Subjects needing discussion were kept track of with pen and paper, re-arranging the urgency of priorities with mutual consent only. Grandpa Baul kept his grandchildren busy with projects and only a slight bit of reconnaissance when deemed necessary. Their inventions were beginning to bear fruit.

As the visit approached its end, a contented and refreshed Mrs. Baul wondered if Sir Peter and Lady Sarah might be just the confidants she needed, to present the thrill of discovering Rev. Baul's double identity. No, on further reflection it was entirely possible that the Radcliffes themselves were wrapped up in something similar, since they were internationally acclaimed and all. Best if things were kept undercover: a secret guarded in capable hands.

Mrs. Baul Investigates

These were unpredictable and dangerous times after all. Mrs. Baul was aware of Felix, a government assigned "listener" in their church service each week. She had also discovered closely monitored telephone and computer lines in the Baul's home and church office. No one had contradicted her conclusions. She even cleverly detected that suspicious secret police had entered their home while they were absent one evening. The Baul family had heard her recount this triumph time and time again. Smoke lingering in the air had been her telltale sign. It most certainly was smoke from a cigarette, not from the burning fields in the Nile Delta.

As Mrs. Baul's investigations became more exacting, she was certain that her husband's frequently used cell phone was an elite satellite phone, most likely including a global positioning system. She'd never seen him disengaged from this phone except for nightly recharging purposes. Her timely examination while he was showering one morning yielded dozens of unrecognizable telephone numbers.

"Joe, do you remember that prayer book your godparents gave you during their last visit?" inquired Grandpa. "Peter confided in me that if their services were ever needed, the capability for contacting them was installed inside."

"Really? That's cool," exclaimed Joe.

"You know how into adventure they are," Grandpa continued. "Nothing would stop them for coming to your aide. I think the time has come to request a favor."

"Why didn't you tell me about this sooner?" asked Joe.

"To be honest with you it slipped my mind until now," admitted Grandpa. "I thought it a bit overly dramatic at the time. You've seen Sir Peter and Lady Sarah in action. I wasn't even sure I really believed him and I definitely didn't think we'd ever have to take up his offer."

"I'll be right back," Joe said as he left in pursuit of his gift.

-9-

The explosion

Morning arrived far too soon for the Baul children following such an animated evening. After some effort the night before, a signal was successfully activated toward the whereabouts of Sir Peter and Lady Sarah. Grandpa was working in his workshop long before breakfast but had not been able to confirm a response. The Radcliffe's receptors were either turned off temporarily or no longer available. It would be helpful to know where they were and if any news had reached them of the Rt. Rev. Edwin Cornwall-McGrath III, a friend they had in common. Absolutely no new leads had been reported on that front in the last 24 hours.

Mrs. Baul was just emerging into the hall in her bathrobe as Miriam and Joseph waved goodbye to her on their way to school; Grandpa would have to investigate on his own that morning. Thankfully it was the last day of school before the long holiday weekend.

Rev. Baul appeared from the garden as Grandpa sat down for breakfast. He was clearly excited about the pigeon competition.

"I am going to be meeting Musa after lunch to discuss more details on the race," Rev. Baul announced, noticing his wife's gloomy mood. "What's the matter, my dear?"

"Oh, I'm just agitated by that miserable nightmare that keeps recurring. I'm sorry to be so distracted. The whole event does sound exciting," Mrs. Baul conceded. "Let alone seeing the exotic oasis and the Great Sand Sea. I'm sure you can guess that visiting the desert frightens me right now with this haunting dream hanging over me."

"I'm so sorry," her husband offered.

Grandpa Baul wisely held his tongue. His son had mentioned the visions disturbing her sleep but there was no point in trying to convince her that she would not drown in a jeep buried in an avalanche of sand. Although never vocalized, Grandpa Baul guessed even the sighting of jeeps around Cairo would spark concern these days.

"If only I could shake the irrational fear it's producing," she continued. "But the dream seems so real. I literally feel my throat constricting and I wake up feeling I'm being strangled by fear as well as sand."

"Maybe it will be good for you to face this trip and then realize it is unfounded? I'll be with you, my love," Rev. Baul reassured her.

Mrs. Baul remained silent while Grandpa wished he could disappear from the conversation and begin his search for the diary.

"Don't forget we have an Oud recital to attend this evening," Rev. Baul cheerfully reminded his wife.

"I do have it on my calendar but I had completely forgotten with the busyness of the week," admitted Mrs.

Baul, shaking off her daze. "Thank you for reminding me."

"Where is it being held?" asked Grandpa Baul before excusing himself.

"In the Mena House hotel gardens next to the Giza pyramids," explained his son. "This is an important charity fundraiser so our presence is expected. That means our weekend plans must be set before sundown." Grandpa seized the moment to excuse himself from breakfast, slipped out of the room and headed toward the library.

"Have you had a chance to arrange the flight to Siwa yet?" asked Mrs. Baul.

"That's first on my list for the day. I'm hoping to get a morning flight plan registered for so we can settle into our lodge by lunchtime and spend the majority of the day exploring the sites."

"What was that?" shrieked Mrs. Baul as she jumped up from her chair as a loud blast shook their kitchen windows. Moments later it sounded like bombs were exploding all around them.

"I think that's just dynamite at the quarry out of town, my love," consoled Rev. Baul, but not looking entirely convinced himself.

"No, it's way too loud and you know it! It must be the children's school. A bomb has exploded! They're under siege!"

"I'm sure it hasn't, dear," Rev. Baul wrapped his wife gently in his arms. "Let me call over to security there and make sure all is well."

"I'm sorry I can't help myself," she apologized with tired bewilderment. So many near misses plagued her day and night. "Please do call for me. That was way too loud to explain away."

As Rev. Baul hurriedly left to call the school, he ran into his father racing back toward the kitchen. Grandpa Baul tried to keep his voice steady for the sake of his daughter-in-law but his eyes betrayed his concern.

"The phone lines are busy," Rev. Baul explained moments later. "I'll go over there myself. You two stay here. I'll let you know as soon as I hear something."

Both very reluctantly agreed. Mrs. Baul assured them she would be fine on her own so Grandpa kindly led the way to her bedroom to ensure she would lie down and rest. She trailed slowly behind him quietly muttering to herself, "and I keep hearing gunfire! Those noises are probably just firecrackers, but I do know I'm onto something real with this donkey business. And that was not dynamite in the quarry."

The clever concealment of Mrs. Baul's diary was a new precaution she had started taking when her private investigations began to accumulate. Apparently she thought securing it within the confines of their own bedroom was too high a risk. As Grandpa carefully pulled the book out of its usual position he noticed several new volumes were resting beside it. He edged them forward slightly. Still distracted by the series of explosions he worked less skillfully than usual but soon was rewarded with the discovery of a significant stash of bundled money and a small but thick manual for a satellite phone.

Cautiously he set the money back into place and hurriedly flipped through the instruction manual to see if by chance his daughter-in-law's phone number was anywhere to be found. It would be much more useful to lay hands on the actual phone, but without his grandchildren as spotters, such an attempt would be too risky. The household staff had been in high preparation to ready the Baul family for their weekend adventure, but now was huddled together discussing the nearby blasts.

Sure enough, there was a number written in her handwriting on the back of the manual. Did it belong to his daughter-in-law or Madame Napoleon? Either would be useful. Hastily Grandpa copied down the number, tucked the handwritten tome between the pages of his newspaper, and disappeared toward his private quarters.

With so much adrenaline racing through her veins Mrs. Baul could not possibly lie down and rest while the lives of her children hung in the balance. Grandpa was eager enough to excuse himself so she took the opportunity to see what was happening on the street from the best vantage point in the house.

In front of the villa's entrance she could see her husband having an animated discussion with the uniformed security guard. But instead of getting straight into his car to drive to school as promised, he stopped to talk to a street sweeper on the street. Soon a garbage collector joined them. What was he doing? This is was no time for niceties. It was impossible these men were in his employ. She made several attempts to call Madame Napoleon but her home telephone was engaged and satellite phone switched off. She jumped when a maid appeared at her door to tell her she had a telephone call in her husband's office. There was only one person who would call her on that second line and it was to be used in case of emergencies only.

"Hello, my friend. I've just heard the news!" boomed the excited voice of Madame Napoleon. "Are you okay?"

"What news? The bomb?"

"No, no my husband just called from the office to tell me the explosion was only some propane gas bottles on the back of a donkey cart," explained Madame Napoleon.

"Oh, thank goodness. A donkey cart? I was sure it was an attack at the kids' school!" Mrs. Baul retorted.

"Yes, I can imagine. But it was just a man on his regular route with a defective bottle. When one blew up it set off the others. No need to worry."

"But what about the donkey and the man, did they survive? Do you think this was just an accident?" probed Mrs. Baul.

"I can't imagine they could survive something like that. In light of everything else that is going on it is tempting to suspect foul play but I really don't think my husband would lead me astray," she answered.

-10-

The papyrus message

"Hello Kubri," Musa heard Rev. Baul say into his cell phone as he arrived on the scene. "Yes, we also got that confirmation on the explosions. The official liftoff in Siwa isn't until early Saturday morning but I have to rush back for church that evening. We'll just meet you there Friday then. So glad you can come."

"I have heard a lot about Kubri these days. Will he be in Siwa this weekend?" ventured Musa as he busied himself with an adjustment on the pigeon transporter he was carrying.

"Yes he will in fact. You've met him before, haven't you?"

"Just briefly once," said Musa.

"He has decided to take the long drive instead of flying with us," shared Rev. Baul. "Some sudden business to sort out up on the Mediterranean Coast but convenient enough as that will put him over half-way to Siwa at that point."

"Is he heading to Alexandria?" Musa probed in as detached a manner as possible.

"No, he said Dabaa or something like that. All those towns run together in my mind," Rev. Baul explained distractedly. "I must go find my wife. She heard the news about the explosions and had to lie down."

"I think I'll drop in and see if Grandpa Baul is around before I head back to the boat. The Coast seems to be the chosen place for Cairo respite in the heat of summer. I have some cousins I'd love to visit up there sometime," he threw in for good measure.

Musa knocked a recognizable rhythm at the entry of Grandpa Baul's workshop.

"Grandpa Baul?" called Musa.

"Yes, is that you Musa?" asked Grandpa as he opened the door and ensured it was firmly shut after him. "Those exploding gas bottles have even put me on edge."

"You're not the only one. I just thought I'd stop by to give you an update," he said. "The research you asked me to do concerning Mrs. Baul's dealings has not turned up anything at all."

"That's good to hear. Your timing is excellent. I've discovered some important information in her journal entries."

"The last time we had to go there we were already way over our heads," Musa recalled.

"We're getting there fast. From what I've read so far, Mrs. Baul is convinced the ever-generous Kubri is leading a terrorist cell in which donkeys play a critical role."

"Donkeys?" asked Musa very confused. "How on earth did her mind reach such a preposterous conclusion?"

"Madame Napoleon no doubt spurred her on," concluded Grandpa. "There will be no stopping her without dramatic safeguards in place."

"I think I'd better bow out of the morning flight and follow Kubri by car," said Musa. "We need to confirm his loyalties and the purpose of his own investigations."

"I can arrange a driver for you," suggested Grandpa. "We can stay in contact through our satellite phones. You better take this mystery phone number I found on Mrs. Baul's satellite phone manual."

"It's her number?" asked Musa.

"Actually I don't know for sure. It must be hers or Madame Napoleon's," explained Grandpa. "Can you deploy the GPS tracking device system, as soon as one of them is on the move?"

"Sure. I know Rev. Baul will be disappointed I'm not going on the chartered flight with him but see if Miriam can help him with any extra pigeon care necessary."

"Excellent suggestion," added Grandpa. "She does love those birds, Cinnamon and Sugar."

"Also, I'll be shocked if Mrs. Baul doesn't pursue this pyramid treasure hunt before we leave for Siwa. She hasn't breathed a word of it to her friend so that makes me all the more sure she's going to take the bait."

"That sounds like reasonable logic for her," agreed Musa. "When do you think she'll head out?"

"I'm guessing this morning. Would you mind following with your tour guide disguise or something?"

"She's never recognized me yet," beamed Musa. "Be happy to. Just let me know when she leaves the house."

"Sure will," replied Grandpa. "Thanks friend."

Musa went on his way to start packing up all the gear they would need for the trip. Grandpa would bring what he could as well since he would need to set up a makeshift surveillance headquarters long before Musa arrived.

"Musa, she's on the move," Grandpa placed his call to the felucca headquarters knowing Musa had probably arrived just shortly before.

"No problem, I'm going to sail over to the other shore so I can beat them to Giza and maybe do a bit of discrete browsing before she arrives."

"Great idea! Keep me posted. Stay safe."

"Will do," Musa replied eagerly.

He slipped into his disguise and pushed his boat out into the current. He polled for a few minutes until he caught the wind just right and was over to western side of the Nile in no time.

Once on sight at the ancient Giza monuments he decided to slip down into the pyramid chamber himself for a good look around. No one else was in view. Tourist season was at a lull after the random bombings around town recently. He climbed down the stretched ladder awkwardly in his slippery sandals and flowing indigo *galabeya*. A long male dress was hardly practical for such an endeavor, although the coolness of the outfit certainly made sense in a desert setting.

He finally reached the bottom rung, adjusted his jostled turban and entered the tourists' tomb. This renovated queen's chamber provided less adventuresome sightseers a glimpse of hieroglyphics and an authentic view of what ancient chambers actually looked like, but without the hassle of the claustrophobic climb inside the Great Pyramid. Musa had brought a flashlight along as a precaution but the room was already well lit. It didn't take him long at all to spot a piece of papyrus crammed into a low crack in one of the corners. He listened to make sure no climbers were about to join him and carefully unfolded the note.

> Mena House concert tonight.
> Will find you.

Musa quickly refolded the note and set it back in place. Just as he reached the top of the ladder he heard the excited voice of Mrs. Baul coming toward him, murmuring to herself. She was unquestionably trying to psych herself up before braving the ladder into the pyramid chamber. He ducked out of the entrance swiftly and took shelter behind an archaeological site nearby. She was definitely alone and not being watched. Musa spotted her taxi driver leaning against his car down in the Sphinx parking lot. It must have taken her a while to find the message because Musa waited nearly twenty minutes before she emerged again. Her expression was animated but surprisingly not full of fear. He'd report back to Grandpa Baul once he reached his boat.

-11-

Joe disappears

As soon as school ended for the day, Joe and Miriam made their way home in eager anticipation of their holiday break. Grandpa was nowhere to be found, but a red flashing light indicated the discovery of a signal from the Radcliffe's high-tech apparatus. The electronic screen embedded in the back cover of Joe's prayer book revealed a coded message of some sort. After a bit of investigation a narrow button in the seam of the book proved to serve as a decoder.

Gaza clinic.
Border open.
Bus ok.
Standing by.

In Grandpa's absence they also tuned in to monitor their mother's new bracelet.

"I have not misplaced it. It is missing. I'm sure of it," Mrs. Baul cried in distress. "What have I done? I should never have trusted the library. Someone is out to get us. This proves it!"

They could only hear mumblings in response.

"I can look again but it's futile. We're ruined," Mrs. Baul whined. "No, the money is still there. These are professionals at work."

"Grandpa must have borrowed her diary as planned," exclaimed Joe.

"Where is he? Where is she?" asked Miriam impatiently.

"I don't know. Just call him," Joe suggested. "Mom must be talking on the phone or we'd be able to hear the other voice clearly."

Their satellite phone was not in its usual place but thankfully the diary was sitting in plain view. They didn't have time to spare. If they could replace it immediately they might avoid further detection. But they were unsure if Grandpa had gleaned all he needed from its pages. They would have to risk it. Miriam stood guard as Joe slipped into the library.

"Hi, Dad," Joe heard Miriam say in an overly loud voice in the hallway.

"Hello, Miriam," said Rev. Baul. "How are you?"

"Okay, thanks," she continued, clearly stalling for time as she heard something thump loudly behind the library door.

"What was that?" her father asked.

"What was what?" asked Miriam.

"Coming from the library, that odd noise."

"Oh that, I think those are just the workers in the garden Dad," Miriam adlibbed. "Maybe they dropped something heavy."

"The garden? I don't remember any work needing done."

"Yes on the fountain, remember?" fibbed Miriam as she quickly carried on. "I'm so glad to find you home, Dad. I have some homework research I need to do over the long weekend and I don't want to take it with me to Siwa."

"I don't blame you. What's the subject?"

"Actually the teacher let us choose anything related to a current event in Egypt and I talked her into letting me cover the pigeon racing," sputtered Miriam as she stretched a bit of truth in light of the need for diversion.

"Pigeon racing? How perfect Miriam! Good for you."

Her father cooperated easily. Miriam hoped Joe had been able to restore the diary and would emerge momentarily with some excuse about library research himself. As the conversation continued Miriam grew concerned at what was keeping her brother. She learned more about racing techniques than she ever imagined possible. After a while conversation lagged and she produced new questions about Cinnamon and Sugar, the pigeons they planned to enter in the race. This line of discussion was actually interesting to her and she momentarily forgot the reason for her original diversion.

"Miriam, do you think you should be writing some of these things down?" asked her father.

"I will, Dad. You've really been helpful," she added. "Are there any books I should read on the subject?"

"I'm certain I have a few on the shelves in here," he mused.

At this point Miriam figured it was wisest to enter the library with her father, as that was obviously his intended destination. She was tired of waiting for Joe and could cover for him herself if she had to. When the library door swung wide open, Miriam was shocked not to find her brother inside. Maybe he'd slipped through the garden window? No, there were bars on all the lower story windows of the villa.

"Look at that pile of fallen books and dust, would you?" Rev. Baul was never happy to see books or piles of anything out of place.

"That's odd," noted Miriam. "Maybe the maid was sweeping up and got interrupted?"

"Could be I suppose, but would she have knocked these books onto the floor?"

"That is strange," acknowledged Miriam. "I'll help you pick them up."

"Thank you. It should be obvious where they go. Don't worry about the dust pile for now," he said before refocusing on his search for pigeon manuals. "Here you go. Exactly what I was looking for."

"Thanks so much, Dad," she said before bowing out politely and zooming back through the garden to headquarters.

"Grandpa!" exclaimed Miriam as she entered the workshop panting for air.

"Miriam, there you are," replied Grandpa. "Where have you been?"

"Where have *you* been?" she echoed as she stopped to catch her breath.

"Big developments to fill you in on," began Grandpa.

"Joe is missing!" yelled Miriam.

"Missing? What do you mean missing?" Grandpa Baul voiced alarm.

"We went to put the diary back in place even though we weren't sure you were done with it because we overheard Mom panicking on the phone about it to Madame Napoleon. Then Dad came walking toward the library just after Joe slipped inside and I must have stalled him for a good fifteen minutes thinking he would come back out with some sort of excuse and he never did."

"Slow down, Miriam. Everything is going to be okay. I'm so sorry to force you to have to create such a diversion in the first place. I had intended to get the diary back in place within minutes, not hours. Did you go inside the library to look for Joe after you finished talking with your dad?"

"Yes, Dad and I went in together and he was nowhere to be found."

"Are you sure he wasn't hiding behind a couch or your dad's desk?"

"I looked. He was gone. The diary was back in place perfectly but he was gone," she cried. "He couldn't have gone out the window."

"You're right, there are bars on them. And there's no way he could have gotten through the door without you seeing him?"

"I was leaning against the door the whole time to prevent Dad from entering," she explained.

"This is very strange. I'm sure there's a logical explanation behind it," assured Grandpa.

"What are we going to do?" asked Miriam.

"We need to get back in there and do a thorough search. Why don't we go back in there together? If your dad is trying to work and we're noisy then he'll clear out, if I'm not mistaken."

"Okay, I told him I was working on a pigeon racing report," Miriam admitted.

"That's a good enough reason to return. I know just where he keeps some of his more interesting books on the subject. He won't mind."

"Did you get a chance to read Mom's diary?" queried Miriam.

"I sure did. Our worst fears were confirmed," Grandpa reported as he shook his head in concern. "I've already filled in Musa on the latest."

Miriam was a bit worried they might encounter her mother in the library as well. But with her heightened suspicions of her husband's activities she was sure to blame him, not them, for the fact that her diary had gone missing. After revealing all to her friend on the telephone, Miriam was certain her mother would head straight back to the library for another confirmation of her woes. If Mrs. Baul found her husband present, his calming demeanor would likely convince her it was simply an oversight on her part. But, if she discovered what Miriam's research project was about she'd be doubly upset at Miriam for embracing her father's pigeon pursuits.

At first their mother had ignored their father's growing pigeon obsession, convinced it would fade if left alone. Yet as time carried on it was clear to all, with the exception of Mrs. Baul, that his pigeons were an enjoyable hobby, not the result of dysfunctional thinking. When the threatening crisis was discussed, her premise dissolved and she began to pursue another line of thinking. What was that line they'd heard her say to Madame Napoleon once? "Since the earliest days of espionage, homing pigeons have been a spy's best friend." The memory of it brought a smile to her face.

"Grandpa, did you know the Radcliffes responded?"

"I saw that when I got back to the workshop," said Grandpa. "That's super news. I dispatched another message myself since Joe wasn't around. Hopefully we'll hear back more quickly this time."

As Miriam and Grandpa walked back through the garden toward the villa, Grandpa filled her in on the latest coastal developments. She couldn't help but glance at the fountain where no repair work was being done.

"You know, Grandpa, there was a very strange noise in the library while Dad and I were talking outside in the hallway."

"What kind of a noise?" probed Grandpa.

"It was like a muted boom, not a loud bang but like something heavy slamming down," explained Miriam.

"That's peculiar. And you're sure it was coming from the library, not outside?"

"Positive," Miriam replied emphatically. "Dad heard it too but Joe had only been inside a minute or two so I thought I needed to stall him longer. I told him it was probably repairs in the garden."

"Did it happen more than once?"

"No just once, but there was also a pile of books that had been bumped off a shelf in one corner and some dusty debris on the floor," she explained. "Dad noticed it too."

"Let's have a good look at it together."

They both arrived just as Rev. and Mrs. Baul were leaving the library, clearly in the midst of a serious discussion. Mrs. Baul's eyes looked a bit red and puffy but Rev. Baul was comforting her with his arm tenderly wrapped around her shoulders. They seemed surprised to run into the two of them but when Miriam flashed her bird book, her father acknowledged her pass to enter and launched into an muffled explanation to his wife.

Grandpa and Miriam looked around the room carefully and called Joe's name as quietly as they could. He was definitely nowhere to be found.

"Miriam, we may have to wait a few minutes until your parents leave for their concert," suggested Grandpa.

"I guess you're right, we can't really start hollering his name at the top of our voices," she acknowledged. "I better go check Joe's room and the rest of the house."

"The household staff will be gone then too," he pointed out. "I think I'll invite Musa over for a visit."

"Darling, we leave for the concert in ten minutes," called Rev. Baul encouragingly.

"Just about ready," Mrs. Baul answered as she stood puzzling over her choice of shoes for the evening. The Oud was one of her husband's favorite Middle Eastern instruments. He had a collection of such antiques creatively displayed in his study. The detailed work put into the mother of pearl inlay on the back of his Syrian acquisition exhibited countless hours of diligent craftsmanship. Several times a year Rev. Baul enthusiastically hosted international school groups and invited local musicians to demonstrate their instruments and musically weave their remarkable histories into the minds of his young guests.

The drive through Cairo that evening was picturesque. A mysterious glow from the setting sun danced on the white limestone of the pyramids looming off in the distance. Traffic was much thinner than usual and the lights lining the Nile River boasted of a city that sparkled to life when the moon made its appearance on the stage of the night sky.

Upon arrival at the Oud concert, Mrs. Baul was unexpectedly introduced to the president of the Donkey Rescue and his attractive wife. At the same moment Madame Napoleon dramatically appeared with her well-known husband gracing her side. Rev. Baul warmly welcomed them all and encouraged further exchange of acquaintances. This was after all a charity fundraising event. Ever tactful, Madame Napoleon and Mrs. Baul interchanged subtle questioning of the Donkey Rescue president. What a coincidence he was present at the recital. Mrs. Baul scanned the crowd for any sign of her messenger but disciplined herself to refocus on the interview at hand.

"Why yes we do have branches about the country," explained the president. "Aswan, Luxor, Alexandria, Siwa."

"Siwa?" queried Mrs. Baul. "How delightful. We are heading there for our first visit tomorrow."

"Well do look up our office if you have time," he encouraged. "It's very near the Temple of Amun. Perhaps Alexander the Great was carried by one of these local four legged ancestors on his renowned trip to Siwa when he was elevated to the status of divine." They all laughed. The story of this event was shrouded with mystery in expatriate circles in Egypt. To be sure the event had held a strong place in tradition as Alexander claims he was pronounced a god, an endorsement required for legitimate rule of the region back then.

"The Oracle of Amun would probably have granted a donkey the title of deity if the price had been right," the president continued, invoking what must have been a well-used joke from the look on his wife's amused face.

"Well, we look forward to learning more about those stories," declared Rev. Baul as dimming lights signaled the concert would begin momentarily. Oblivious to alternate agendas in play, Rev. Baul found their seats and anticipated the haunting quarter-tones of Middle Eastern melodies.

"Very nice to meet you," Mrs. Baul nodded as she excused herself and stealthily winked a conspiratorial eye in Madame Napoleon's direction. Her gesture was instantly understood and both women sought out the restroom before finding their seats.

"Are we set for tomorrow?" queried Mrs. Baul in a flush of excitement.

"I hope so. The fingerprints are in process as we speak!" Madame Napoleon explained after carefully scanning the stalls behind her. "I won't leave before I have those results in hand."

"Good. I also must fill you in on a development I should have mentioned earlier but I wasn't sure if it would endanger you."

"I know exactly what you're going to say," interrupted Madame. "The Giza message?"

"But how did you know?" asked Mrs. Baul in a complete state of shock.

"I arranged that ploy myself dear,"

"But I don't understand!" Mrs. Baul tried hard to keep her heated voice at a whisper.

"I was very concerned to see if anyone was onto our game," she explained. "So I sent you that message to see if someone was listening to our conversations or following you."

"What? How could you do that to me knowing how sensitive I am about dangerous encounters? I thought we were on to something!" Mrs. Baul moaned.

"We are on to something and that's why the precaution was necessary," she continued. "I was very pleased to see that absolutely no one is tracking our movements."

"I suppose that is good news," affirmed Mrs. Baul. "I just wish you had let me in on it ahead of time. I could have played the part."

"I felt it better this way in case professionals were involved."

"We must get to our seats," said Mrs. Baul. "I'll be on my satellite phone but my family doesn't have any idea I own such a gadget. Give me a missed call and I'll get back to you as soon as I possibly can."

"Perfect. *Bon courage* my friend," said Madame. "I am so sorry if I startled you. Please forgive me. I will see you in Siwa."

The lights flickered their final warning.

Musa arrived within moments of the Baul's departure for the concert.

"Hi, Musa!" called Miriam as she descended the rounded marble stairway.

"Thanks for coming. Joe is definitely not anywhere else in the house, Grandpa."

"I rechecked the workshop as well," Grandpa reported.

The three investigators entered the library armed with flashlights and loud voices. They brought Musa up to speed on the mysterious details and Miriam pointed out the fact that the pile of dusty debris had been removed since their last visit. All three voices started shouting Joe's name in unison and almost immediately they heard a familiar coded knock coming from within a corner bookshelf.

"Where is he?" asked Miriam, full of relief at hearing the well-known tapping.

"He's got to be inside the bookshelf behind that corner chair," declared Musa.

"This is the spot where the books were lying on the floor earlier," Miriam walked to the exact location and knelt down.

"Let's get the books back off the shelves and take a look," said Grandpa still puzzled but clearly relieved that his grandson was somewhere nearby.

"Joe, if you can hear me knock twice," yelled Grandpa. A confirming double tap came through loud and clear.

"How did you get inside?" Grandpa yelled again.

"Step on the bottom shelf," came a muffled reply.

"Okay, stand clear Joe," called Grandpa. "Here we go."

Grandpa pushed down on a lever he found concealed at the back of the bottom corner shelf. Slowly the back panel of the wooden shelf began to creak and slowly swung away from them like a door.

"Joe, you're safe," yelled Miriam as she peered in through the darkness and dragged her brother out. She welcomed him with a huge hug after he squeezed himself through an empty shelf.

"You had us scared to death Joe," cried Grandpa as he held his grandson tightly.

"Thanks for getting me out of there!" said Joe as he started wiping cobwebs from his hair and shaking off the dust onto his father's prized camel leather chair. "I was starting to get a bit worried."

"How on earth did you find that secret room?" asked Musa.

"I was trying to hide from Dad behind this chair because I heard him coming and didn't want to be caught until I'd figured out a reason for being here," he explained. "So I dove behind the chair and stumbled into the bookshelf. The next thing I knew the whole panel was opening up!"

"How did you get it to close after you?" Grandpa asked.

"I don't know," he admitted. "I crawled through and was surprised to find I could stand up straight. When I stepped into the passage then the door started to close behind me. I didn't know what to do but I could see light down the tunnel so I figured I'd be okay."

"Tunnel?" the rescuers asked together.

"Yeah it's really cool," said Joe. "It must run under the garden because right in the middle of it where the light was shining through it was wet like something dripped in from above from time to time."

"The fountain?" proposed Miriam.

"It could be that," agreed Joe. "Or maybe even some place where the gardener waters."

"I think you may be right on the fountain idea, Miriam," affirmed Grandpa.

"That would be the kind of structure that would let light through if there were cracks between the tiles," suggested Musa.

"That makes sense," Joe added.

"Where were you when we tried calling to you after Dad and Mom left the room?" asked Miriam.

"I must have been down the passage exploring," explained Joe. "I heard them talking in muffled voices for a while but I knew you'd come find me eventually so I wasn't going to risk being heard."

"Have you ever looked at the architectural design of the villa, Grandpa Baul?" asked Musa.

"No, why?"

"I'm just wondering if this tunnel connects all the way to your guesthouse out back," Musa deliberated.

"That would be cool!" exclaimed Joe. "I would have searched further but I didn't have a flashlight with me."

"Can we try looking, Grandpa?" asked Miriam eagerly.

"What is the structure like, Joe?" asked Musa. "Is it made of dirt or concrete?"

"It's solid concrete. There wasn't any dirt on the edges, just tons and tons of dust and creepy crawling things" Joe carried on dramatically.

"If you think that's going to stop me you're wrong," said Miriam. "Maybe it's like the Baron's Hindu looking palace here in Cairo. We took a field trip there a few years ago."

"That is a cool building," agreed Joe. "We went there too and it's got to be one of the most out of place looking things around. The guy had a tunnel built under ground to connect his palace to a nearby church."

"Didn't he build it on a type of turnstile that would rotate the whole building so that its windows were always facing the sun?" asked Musa.

"It might have moved when it was built a hundred years ago," Miriam conceded.

"Where are Dad and Mom?" asked Joe.

"They've gone to a concert for a couple hours so we're safe," explained Miriam.

"Joe, why don't you lead the way, and Musa you follow?" suggested Grandpa. "Miriam and I will stay here to make sure you can get back out. There must be a way to work the lever from the inside."

"Okay," Joe agreed eagerly as he took his sister's flashlight.

"I'm not sure I can hold my long body up enough to get through," said Musa.

The minute Joe stepped into the passage the panel began to swing shut before Musa could wriggle through. As soon as the door closed fully it began to reopen. Joe had discovered a brass panel at the entrance of the tunnel that closed the door as soon as it was stepped on. With his flashlight he was easily able to find the lever on the tunnel's ceiling that when pulled, reopened the door from the inside.

"Cool!" yelled Joe.

"Can I try, Grandpa?" asked Miriam.

"Sure go ahead. Musa, you join the expedition too. I'll stay here and guard the entrance," Grandpa decided.

The three explorers disappeared down the passage but stepped carefully over the entry section so the bookshelf access area remained open. They relayed information back to Grandpa Baul as they went. By the time they reached the end of the passageway their voices had faded into murmurs.

"Hey Grandpa Baul," called Musa returning down the tunnel. "I definitely think the other end of this burrow comes up into your bungalow."

"Really?" Grandpa's voice was excited. "What does the exit look like?"

"I left the kids exploring further down the tunnel. I'll be back in a minute with more details."

A long period of silence followed. Grandpa called down the passage but didn't receive a response until the familiar rap on the windowpane.

"Hey Grandpa!" Joe and Miriam were jumping up and down at the garden window and behind them stood dark tall Musa with a wide grin on his face. Grandpa hurried over and opened up the window.

"Where's the exit?" he called out eagerly.

"Underneath the huge wooden desk in your office!" announced Joe.

"You're kidding? That old heavy antique?"

"Brilliant construction," admired Musa. "Not the kind of furniture anyone would ever move. It's actually attached to the wall to ensure its concealment."

"Let me close up here and join you," Grandpa Baul said as he shut the library window and went to erase evidence of their evening's adventure.

-12-

Coastal developments

Thursday morning arrived and the Baul family entourage had packed themselves onto a chartered plane to Siwa by late morning. Mrs. Baul sat in a nervous daze in her seat after Rev. Baul subtly reassured her that their pilot was a competent captain and longtime friend. Their flight plan had been delayed by several hours due to locust swarms moving methodically through the wilderness between the Mediterranean Coast and Cairo. Grandpa Baul had discretely ensured that the ecolodge they would be staying at was the same one their friend the Right Reverend had chosen. That would make their search for more information as natural and simple as possible.

As anticipated, Rev. Baul looked visibly disappointed at the news Musa would not be joining them until the following day. It would be a long ten-hour drive for him but all understood the importance of family and his desire to spend an evening visiting his cousins on the coast.

The flight west was very enjoyable in a small aircraft. Twists and turns of ancient caravan routes could easily be seen in all directions throughout the arid land beneath them. The Northern Sahara connected the Mediterranean coastline to central Africa through its all-important network of oases. Siwa was one of the best known due to its role throughout the centuries.

Time yawned on while Grandpa rattled through a narration of Siwan history, battling against the dull roar of jet engines. Apparently when Alexander the Great appeared at Siwa in 331BC he and his soldiers had survived a dangerous desert march. Lush, fertile beauty welcomed them, shady groves of palms and subterranean springs with pure water that had resurfaced after traversing the continent, from Central African tropical forest rains.

The Oracle of Amun had dramatically confirmed Alexander's self-imagined identity as a divine apparition, very expected of such influential rulers. Grandpa couldn't resist expounding his loosely documented theory that the Oracle, a Siwan high priest, upon meeting Alexander greeted him with the words *"O, paidion,"* meaning "Oh, my son," but mispronounced the Greek as *"O, pai dios"* meaning "Oh, son of god," much to Alexander's delight and amazement.

Grandpa skipped ahead to the previous century. 1926 had seen three days and nights of torrential rainfall that pummeled the salt-caked mud houses of Shali, the old town, melting it into mere ruins. During World War II, Siwa sheltered Allied troops from England, Australia and New Zealand with its fresh water springs, Cleopatra's own being the most sought out. Even Field Marshal Rommel made an appearance at one point. However, the Italians who had occupied Libya eventually bombed Siwa "killing 100 people and a donkey."

Mrs. Baul flinched at the pronouncement of the anonymous donkey's death.

"How very odd that history should take notice of a donkey," she declared.

"Yeah," agreed Joe shaking off his drowsiness.

"Well, you know even our Scriptures remember Jesus and his triumphal donkey ride into Jerusalem," interjected Rev. Baul.

"Still it seems to bear significance," insisted Mrs. Baul.

"Do they have camels in Siwa, Grandpa?" asked Miriam in an attempt to change the subject.

"Actually it looks like there are mostly just donkeys," explained Grandpa. "I'm sure these days they bring in camels for the small tourist industry, but jeeps or donkeys are the most common mode of transport, according to what I've read."

Madame Napoleon arranged as early a departure as possible that morning. Her driver repeatedly mentioned the red locust swarms tormenting the road north to Alexandria. At least it was not sandstorm season. That drive could be unbearable when minuscule grains of whirling Sahara squeezed their way into closed car vents, and innocent eyes and lungs. Before leaving the city Madame was able to corroborate results of the fingerprint investigations. When her source from the EU appeared in person on her front doorstep she swiftly ushered him into a sitting room. Thankfully her husband had flown off to Europe for business in the still darkened hours of the morning.

"Madame Napoleon, nothing at all suspicious has shown up for either set of prints you gave me," reported her liaison with a definitive explanation.

"Are you entirely certain?" she asked, a bit deflated in posture.

"Absolutely. We have cross checked our global networks and both men are upstanding global citizens," he explained.

"But what about Kubri's father and his Giza connections? No radical Al-Qaeda connections?" she probed further.

"His father is known for non-violent promotions of peace treaties among the Sinai Bedouin tribes," he countered. "Egypt has honored his leadership and EU peacekeepers have sought his counsel. He and his sons have been bridge builders. There is nothing on our radars to suggest otherwise."

"Thank you for your expertise," Madame Napoleon gathered herself up with effort and courteously disciplined her demeanor to conceal her persistent reservations.

An hour later, completely absorbed in her own thoughts, Madame Napoleon's car pulled out of her driveway, oblivious to the fact that others would be intently trailing her. There was simply nothing of consequence to report to Mrs. Baul. Perhaps in the hours ahead some new evidence would unfold. She would hate to dishearten her friend and discourage their efforts. Still the fear factor remained.

Not an hour from Cairo's outskirts Kubri's hired driver began to murmur. The pace they were traveling kept them a comfortable distance behind Madame's car.

"Look at those dark clouds looming on the horizon," Madame Napoleon pointed out to her driver with great trepidation. "I can't believe it has been seventeen years since such locust storms have visited Egypt."

"I hope they don't keep swarming toward us, Madame. If we find ourselves in the midst of them they could instantly knock our vehicle out of commission."

"But really the chances of that are extremely minimal, aren't they?" she asked her driver for confirmation. "The locusts' winged routes can be seen and anticipated for miles in advance. Maybe we need to put off the road for a bit?"

Traveling perhaps only a half-mile behind, Musa was troubled by similar thoughts. As he emerged from the city's network of static he had engaged his GPS tracker. The satellite phone number Rev. Baul had procured definitely did not belong to Madame Napoleon. Musa felt quite free to follow Kubri as closely as necessary. He had only met him once briefly at Rev. Baul's downtown café, so the chances of being recognized as a passenger in a following car were negligible.

Suddenly, Madame Napoleon screamed, "Stop the car! The locusts!"

"Sorry Madame," cried her driver as he skillfully spun the wheel in the direction they were skidding and regained control of the vehicle. Darkness had momentarily overtaken them with a cloud of large buzzing red wings. One moment they had been far off in the distance; the next they were bearing down wreaking a path of destruction.

"Oh dear, look at the car behind us! Should we stop and help them?" she asked.

"It looks like someone is pulling over. It's a miracle an accident was avoided," said the driver. "At the speeds we travel this road, there are fatal accidents daily. I would never risk your life after dark on these roads, Madame."

"Thank you. I feel quite shaken. I've never seen anything like it. Imagine being in the midst of an ancient Egyptian plague!" she exclaimed.

Unsure how to counter such a statement, her driver distracted her with a calming observation: "It looks like the car behind us will be fine. They've only hit a pile of bricks. No human harm done."

"Kubri, are you okay?" yelled Musa unafraid of detection as he ran toward the steaming car that had swerved off the road.

"I'm fine. Is my driver okay?" he asked quickly. "How do you know my name?"

"I am Musa, Rev. Baul's employee," he explained.

"Of course. I recognize you now," Kubri confirmed as he began to assess the damage done. A low makeshift stack of bricks had ploughed through the front of the car.

"Mr. Kubri," called his driver. "I am hurt."

By then Musa's driver had appeared and come to the aid of Kubri's driver. He spoke to him in rapid but soothing Arabic and decided to flag down the next minivan. He knew of a medical clinic not far off the road that would be able to treat him. At worse his collarbone was broken but clearly the pain was excruciating.

"I am so sorry, my friend. We will get you good help," Kubri empathetically assured his driver.

"Your car is totaled," observed Musa. "Where are you heading? I would be happy to have you join me."

"How kind of you," replied Kubri. "If I can arrange for proper care for my driver I will take you up on your generous offer."

An uncommonly empty minivan pulled off the main road shortly. For the right price the driver was elated to be hired and would ensure good care was found. He knew immediately of the clinic Musa's driver described and would wait and then shuttle him home to his family. Kubri had obviously paid him a generous sum and gave his driver additional funds as well. He would call the man's family and explain the situation.

If it hadn't been for the urgency of his errand, Kubri would have stayed and taken the driver himself. However, because the injury was not life threatening, Kubri sent him on his way and sincerely thanked Musa for coming to his aid. He also placed a call to arrange for his damaged car to be towed back to Cairo to await his return.

Back in pursuit of Madame Napoleon, Musa figured she was at least thirty minutes ahead of them by now.

"Musa, I have to be honest with you," began Kubri. "I am on a mission to protect your Rev. Baul from disaster."

"What?" Musa asked quite shocked. "You too?"

"The mind of a beautiful woman, my *Gameelah*, can be a very dangerous thing," he smiled with affection.

The men stared at each other, recognizing an unfolding plot whose central purpose they shared. Kubri was the first to expose details he'd discovered. He had suspected from the start that their innocent Rev. Baul had his hands full beyond measure. His certainties had been confirmed when his cousin had disclosed the fact that Madame Napoleon had sent his own and Rev. Baul's fingerprints to the EU laboratories. The assumptions behind such a request threatened exposure to the press at large. Thankfully Kubri was able to forestall such a leak and convince his cousin as to the warped yet innocent meddling of Mrs. Baul and her friend. Assuredly Egypt did not want problems with the international community and Kubri was given authority to set things straight without delay.

Musa shook his head in bewilderment and filled Kubri in on the larger web of conclusions—the missing bishop, donkeys, and weapons of mass destruction. He shared Grandpa Baul's sound instinct to trust Kubri. Such full disclosure from Kubri now was the final proof Musa needed to give him the license to join forces in the cause. As the hours passed by, the two men put a plan into place that would demand the unknown cooperation of Madame Napoleon. She would of course discover no weapons of mass destruction in El-Dabaa and no donkeys crossing the border from Libya illegally. They would shadow her carefully and let things play out. Mrs. Baul was perhaps a greater concern.

In time Kubri and Musa's route found them at a T-junction on the Mediterranean Coast, where World War II history was commemorated with an internationally funded monument and museum. They turned at El-Alamein to travel due west and soon found themselves approaching the outskirts of El-Dabaa.

Musa asked his driver to slow down and search for the old nuclear plant facilities. Their car came to a halt near a wide stretch of fenced land. Military guarded the perimeter, making the entry quite obvious, but warning signs blocked access. No sign of any activity. Armed at a safe distance with binoculars, both men spotted Madame Napoleon's car. Her driver was leaning against the side of the car taking a cigarette break while Madame Napoleon was pacing about searching the ground.

"What is she looking for?" asked Musa.

"Clues," proposed Kubri.

"Donkey droppings," Musa exclaimed.

"Of course," agreed Kubri. "And no stables anywhere to be seen. How devastated she'll be."

"She looks a bit disillusioned already. Looks like she's getting out her phone. I would love to hear her breaking the news to Mrs. Baul," grinned Musa.

"Poor ladies. Let's hope they close down their efforts once and for all."

"Not likely," added an experienced Musa.

"Look Musa! She hasn't given up. It looks like she's going to try to get inside!"

"What? How would she have the authority to do that?" asked Musa.

"I wouldn't put anything past her," noted Kubri.

"Now what do we do?"

"If she can get her way in that easily then I think this official document my cousin procured for me will be just the trick we need," Kubri stated.

"Document?"

"Yes, as a precaution I asked him for a signed, stamped and sealed letter of introduction on my behalf," explained Kubri. "I was hoping I wouldn't have to use it except in an emergency, but this looks like as good a time as any."

"I doubt they'll let me in with you," said Musa.

"Let's just say you're my business associate and see what happens," suggested Kubri.

"Lead the way!"

Both men were stopped at the entrance, but the gates opened wide when the guards saw the seal of the Secret Police. The expansive grounds inside the nuclear compound looked barren and completely deserted.

"Where did she disappear to?" whispered Musa.

"Look, there's another foreigner on the premises," pointed out Kubri discretely.

They decided to approach the other man and found out he was a European journalist just snooping around as a follow up to the latest stories in the international news. On task with their official business concerns, Kubri requested a tour of the grounds. No steam was rising from any of the dilapidated buildings so production had obviously not been resumed. Musa's phone rang loudly and a guard rushed toward them.

"You can't answer that here," panicked Kubri.

"Sorry, I'm turning it off."

The guard attempted to confiscate his phone but Kubri stood his ground with authority and assured him it was turned off and it would not happen again. Eventually they spotted Madame Napoleon walking around the inside perimeter of the compound, most likely still searching for donkey dropping clues. She never attempted to enter any of the buildings and as soon as she left the area Kubri and Musa tactfully excused themselves with promises that the higher-ups would be pleased to hear of the plant's cooperation.

"Well, that seemed conclusive," noted Musa the minute they were outside the intimidating walls.

"There's no way even those women can stay on course with their current line of thinking," concluded Kubri. "Looks like she's calling you know who again."

"Let's hang back a bit and I'll see who tried to call me."

"Musa?" a voice broke through the phone.

"Yes, who is this?" he asked.

"Peter Radcliffe," came an eager reply.

"Sir Peter! What an honor," Musa answered. "I'm so sorry I had to hang up on you earlier. I hadn't heard if you would be able to join us for sure."

"Certainly will be. Coming along the coast on a bus across the Sinai. We are scheduled to go past Alexandria to Marsa Matruh before heading south," he explained.

"Why don't we meet you in Marsa Matruh and take you the rest of the way?" suggested Musa.

"Splendid," he agreed.

Exact arrangements were made with the Radcliffes. Then Musa called Grandpa by satellite phone and surprised him with news of their newfound confidant, Kubri. Grandpa Baul had discretely answered his phone in a grove of palm trees surrounding the family's picnic lunch spot. He assured them all was well. Rev. Baul seemed in heaven as he doted on his happy wife who was drinking in the beauty of fresh air and wide-open spaces. She had mentioned her desire to visit the Donkey Rescue but no firm plans had been set.

Minutes later Miriam and Joe noticed their mother had gone missing. A short search found her squatting behind a resting donkey cart with a confused and disappointed look on her face, as she listened earnestly to her phone.

-13-

Donkey carts

Rev. Baul took his family back to their ecolodge for an afternoon siesta, seeing that vacation allowed for such luxuries. He announced his plan to let them rest while he officially registered his pair of pigeons for the race. He would do a bit of probing for the missing trekkers as well, on behalf of Bishop Kareem, but no sense in worrying his wife with news of his involvement.

"Miriam. Joseph," called Mrs. Baul. "May I speak to you for a moment before you go rest?"

"Sure," answered Joe.

"Come into my room," suggested Miriam as she watched Grandpa scurry off toward his own. Joe and Grandpa were sharing a room, which was set up as a makeshift monitoring station, but Miriam purposely had nothing incriminating in hers.

"I don't want to alarm either of you," began their mother with a sense of urgency, "but I think it's time I let you in on a few secrets. I definitely don't want your father or grandfather to be aware of anything I reveal."

"Okay, what's up?" asked Miriam.

"I can only give you a rough sketch of what's going on right now because time is short," their mother began. "You know the kidnapped bishop that everyone has been talking about? Well I am certain I can find his whereabouts."

"Near here?" asked Joe.

"I think so," she continued. "He is most likely being held hostage because he must have stumbled onto crucial information that threatened to expose an international terrorist ring at work. I am guessing their headquarters are in Siwa and under the cover of the Donkey Rescue mission."

"The Donkey Rescue mission?" asked Miriam. "But they're helping donkeys and the livelihood of people, aren't they?

"Time will tell," concluded their mother. "And it may be dangerous," she added.

Nothing was said of donkey smuggling or weapons of mass destruction. The children were mildly surprised that she was still in hot pursuit after what they assumed Madame Napoleon had found during her coastal exploration. They also realized she was in desperate straits to be taking either of them into her confidence. It would be just the open door they needed to hone in on her scheme. The Baul trio had predicted the arrival of Madame Napoleon at some point during the night.

"You will both have to be up for adventure if you want to join me," cautioned Mrs. Baul.

"Sounds good to me," said Joe eagerly.

"Me too," Miriam agreed.

"I have arranged to borrow some *tarfottets*, you know the long gray cotton dresses you see here embroidered with green and orange hues of colored silk?" Mrs. Baul outlined the details of her plan. "Joseph, I know the men wear *galabeyas* but we will need full disguises. Luckily all the local village women completely cover their heads with long black veils so no one will be able to take notice of our foreignness."

"You want me to walk around like that?" Joe's alarmed voice quivered.

"No dear. I've hired a donkey and cart. That's how people travel around here unless they are taking tourists out to the desert in jeeps or with camels. I prefer camels, personally," she clarified. "We will be going to visit the Donkey Rescue charity headquarters here."

"Why can't we just go visit it as tourists or volunteers?" asked Miriam impulsively before determining further questions could jeopardize their involvement.

"I wish this were a charity visit but it isn't. There is something suspicious going on. We must investigate the compound and track down the kidnapped bishop," she pronounced. "Surely no one else seems to be coming to the dear man's rescue. I may need your help with speaking Siwi, Miriam, if things come to that."

"I only know the basics," she pointed out.

"You'll do just fine, dear. No speaking may be necessary," smiled her mother. "Disguises should be delivered within the next ten minutes. I'll bring them to you in the concealed bags I've requested and then let's meet out behind the lodge twenty minutes after that. I've taken every precaution I can think of to keep you out of harm's way."

"Okay," Miriam and Joe agreed.

"Let's synchronize our watches," proposed Mrs. Baul.

"Sure," they agreed, not quite certain that was necessary.

"Thank you both for your help. I'll send you a signal soon," added their mother as she left the room.

"This is wild!" exclaimed Joe the minute she was gone. "I sure hope Grandpa tuned in for this one." Miriam laughed at the image of her brother, let alone her mother, in such inspired camouflage.

"We better go check-in with Grandpa and see what he's thinking," Miriam suggested. "I know this missing bishop is a serious affair, but I doubt this is the way to do a search and rescue."

"I'm with you there," agreed Joe. "But I think she's looking harder for weapons of mass destruction than for her old British friend."

"It does look that way," said Miriam as they left to talk to their grandfather.

They found Grandpa on the telephone with the hotel manager who knew Musa. Grandpa ushered them in quickly. The only reasonable interpretation as to why Mrs. Baul would go to such lengths had to be that she still suspected to find weapons of mass destruction; otherwise why such extreme measures? The children agreed. Any repercussion to being caught in such disguises was the only dangerous element in her latest scheme.

"The only way I'm going to allow these ridiculous plans to move forward is if I'm following behind you myself."

"But you'll stand out like a sore thumb, Grandpa," Joe pointed out.

"I will suitably cover myself," he explained. "And I'll be in constant verbal contact through Miriam's *hijaab* which I happened to bring along."

"That's a great idea Grandpa," said Miriam.

"The *hijaab* can easily be concealed beneath the garb your mother gives you," explained Grandpa. "Musa's further engineering efforts on the simultaneous translation angle were put on hold when the Siwa trip was announced. But using it just as a two-way monitoring device will come in handy now."

"Hey I want to try it out," said Joe.

"You'll have plenty to worry about yourself Joe," noted Grandpa who couldn't constrain a rumbling chuckle in his voice.

The long bumpy ride toward Donkey Rescue headquarters soon jarred the emotional state of a perspiring Mrs. Baul.

"How much longer do you think it will be, Joseph?" asked his bold but irritated mother.

"I have no idea," whispered Joe in as high a voice as he could muster.

Miriam laughed to herself and looked back at her grandfather. She could not resist the temptation to snap a few discrete photos of him in his own beautifully hand-woven *tarfottet*. The evidence would be worth the guaranteed burst of aggravation it would later arouse.

Eventually settling into a jostling rhythm, the travelers engaged the scenes of Siwa through screened webs of material: palm groves, fresh water baths, sugar cane fields and wildflowers. Barefooted children darted out in front of their carts playing with homemade toys. As invisible as they were to life around them, Mrs. Baul grew more and more anxious as the journey progressed.

"Miriam, I know our driver speaks some English but if you could take over communications that would put me more at ease," explained Mrs. Baul. "Can you confirm our instructions that once we arrive all we want him to do is drop us at the road entrance and wait for us to return?"

"No problem," responded Miriam as she inched her way forward. She knew the driver had been promised a good wage and would not question any discrepancies in her Siwi accent. Grandpa was on alert to stop his driver and cart on a moment's notice. The shoulder high grass surrounding them would provide ample cover for accessing the property.

At last their donkey cart veered to the right and came to a stop at the edge of a grove of tall dusty date palms. Mrs. Baul's primary objective became obvious quickly.

"Children, I want you to look for suspicious buildings that could cleverly conceal the whereabouts of a kidnapped bishop," their mother announced with commanding force.

Miriam and Joe set off on their assignment as a team.

"Her mission looks obvious," Joe commented.

"You mean her private search for evidence of manufactured goods?" asked Miriam.

"Yeah, no ordinary donkey stables would be able to camouflage large-scale weaponry fabrication," noted Joe.

An initial perusal of the grounds produced no indication whatsoever of anything problematic in nature. An undeterred Mrs. Baul even peered inside a dilapidated outbuilding at the sound of a braying donkey and emerged with a grimace on her face. She briskly announced the quest as inconclusive and motioned for their driver to help them remount before retracing their route.

Just as Mrs. Baul was climbing into the back of the cart she noticed deep wide tire tracks in dry mud leading off the edge of the dirt road. No grass had been disturbed so the trail went cold immediately. Even under the cover of veils, both Miriam and Joe observed the change in their mother's demeanor. As they neared the end of the return journey, Mrs. Baul took great pains to warn her children again that not a word of their venture was to be shared.

Grandpa Baul breathed a huge sigh of relief as he gathered his grandchildren into his room for debriefing. Miriam laughed the loudest but neither Grandpa nor Joe could resist joining her. She downloaded her photos as the debriefing session began.

"Mom is off her rocker," declared Joe.

"I can't believe it," said Miriam. "Just when you think she can't possibly take things one more step she's off and racing in another direction."

"I wouldn't have believed it if I hadn't seen it with my own two eyes" Grandpa grinned. "I wish we knew what motivated such grandiose ideas. I'm afraid your mother is sinking in quicksand. I've discreetly engaged the hotel staff to keep us aware of her movements and the arrival of any unexpected visitors," explained Grandpa. "The manager said she's hired two camels for a sunrise excursion. I'm not surprised she is going for four legged rather than four wheel drive transport."

"We know who the second rider will be," announced Miriam.

"How does she plan to explain that one to Dad?" asked Joe.

"She'll come up with a clever invention, you just watch," Grandpa said.

"It doesn't take much to divert your trusting father. I'm curious to see how things play out with Sir Peter and Lady Sarah. Their help tomorrow will be crucial."

"Do you really think Mom is trying to track down the missing bishop?" asked Joe.

"Yes, I do," confirmed Grandpa. "That and a terrorist cell and weapons of mass destruction to boot."

"We know Dad is supposed to be hot on that trail too," said Miriam.

"I can't believe no one has found the bishop yet," said Joe.

"I really think it may be as simple as a desert breakdown," mused Grandpa. "I need to make some more inquiries along that line and see what sort of search and rescue efforts have actually been put into action."

"Time will tell," added Miriam.

"It's too weird that Dad and Mom know the bishop though," said Joe. "Dad told me the Radcliffes knew him too from universities days or something like that."

"It is a small world sometimes," agreed Grandpa. "The lodge manager recommended an excellent guide who has agreed to take us around for the weekend in his jeep. Apparently he knows the desert like the back of his hand."

"Will we all fit?" asked Joe.

"Yes, he has a big covered back with benches over the wheel frames. I'll see if I can convince Musa and Kubri to occupy your father while we three head out together. They'll probably be happy for a bit of a break after their long car ride today. Let's start organizing what we'll need for our expedition tomorrow."

"How is that photo for a new screen saver?" beamed Miriam at the display of their documented surveillance event.

"Humph. That looks like blackmail material to me," groaned Grandpa.

"She can't prove it's you inside all that cloth, though," pointed out Joe.

"What about Sir Peter and Lady Sarah, where will they stay?" asked Miriam.

"I've taken the liberty of reserving the room next door to us for Sir Peter and Lady Sarah. Your father would already have taken care of Musa and Kubri. We'll need to talk with them too and see if they should join us or work another angle."

"When are we going to let Dad in on their visit?" queried Joe.

"I don't know," admitted Grandpa. "Any suggestions?"

"Maybe we can tell him we wanted to surprise him for the pigeon race?" suggested Miriam.

"Mom might fall for that but I doubt Dad would," Joe pointed out.

"It could go either way," said Grandpa. "Your mother might think her conspiracy theories all the more confirmed at the sight of them. We need to keep them apart as long as possible."

"Great," said Miriam. "How does she keep all these twists and turns straight? My head is spinning just trying to anticipate her moves."

"Mr. Musa, the car in front of us has missed the turn-off south toward Siwa," announced their driver.

"What?" Musa looked concerned.

"Maybe they're wanting to rest in Marsa Matruh?" suggested Kubri.

"No sir, that exit is just here on the right," pointed out the driver.

"Unbelievable," groaned Musa.

"There's a sign posted for Sidi Barani and Sallum," said Kubri.

"Sallum is right near the Libyan border. Shall I carry on straight then?" asked the driver.

"Yes, please do," decided Musa. "We have plenty of time before our rendezvous with the Radcliffes."

"I agree," said Kubri. "I'd sure rather stop to stretch my legs and eat something, but we better stay with the pursuit."

"What lengths Madame Napoleon will go to," commented Musa.

"She's bound to find donkeys being shuttled across the border," observed Kubri.

"True. I wonder if she will be looking for something specific? Grandpa Baul told me he overheard the ladies discuss your donkey painting," explained Musa. "Mrs. Baul's big clue was the kind of basket the donkey was carrying. She was convinced it wasn't from Egypt but from the North African Maghreb. That led to the search for weapons of mass destruction, history to you now."

"But what do you think she'll do if she sees foreign looking donkey baskets?" asked Kubri.

"I have no idea."

In the clear blue sky above them Musa caught sight of a kit of racing pigeons flying together.

"See those birds up there Kubri?" Musa pointed them out. "They are probably involved in a training toss."

"Is that what you and Rev. Baul do with your pigeons?"

"Yes, it gives them exercise and practice in finding their way home," explained Musa. "Birds of prey are the main hazard these pigeons encounter. I don't see any soaring around right now, only gulls competing for airspace.

Musa explained his preferred theory that racing pigeons relied on the earth's magnetic field to find their way home. However, successful long-distance treks were doomed without diligent training at increased increments of distance from home. Kubri learned that most fanciers guard their training secrets closely. Some will reveal their basic strategy but few will share the details of their success. Always conditioning was key.

Kubri enjoyed the conversation thoroughly during what seemed an endless drive. Seeing Musa so passionate about the subject increased his eagerness to see it all in action soon. Kubri's grandfather had passed down many stories of revered ancestors who were involved in the sport of birding in one form or another but he'd never witnessed a pigeon race.

"The border is just ahead, Mr. Musa," exclaimed their driver.

"Just keep a safe distance behind them. There will be a lot of military guards around so we won't be able to use our binoculars," explained Musa.

"Look, she's pulling over toward the beach dunes," observed Kubri.

Their car quickly turned off the main road as well and stopped its engine on the shoulder of the road. All three gentlemen got out, opened up the hood of the car and peered inside. They had bought themselves as much time as needed. Kubri got out his phone and called his cousin as promised. He reported with relief the El-Dabaa developments on the other end of the line. His cousin offered to step in with border officials if necessary but Kubri assured him they had reached yet another harmless dead end.

Madame Napoleon's driver got out with purpose and marched up to the main road. He looked both directions and started walking toward a group of guards on duty about a hundred yards further west. Madame made her way to the edge of the road as well, stepping carefully over dry brush and dark patches of tar; a huge orange hat shaded her face as she stared toward the border off in the distance.

Passing traffic was sporadic in both directions. Only one basketless donkey was attached to a cart and loaded with freshly picked vegetables. Its master was prodding his four-legged companion toward the crossing, apparently hoping to sell his wares on Libyan soil. Seemingly unsatisfied and a bit uneasy, Madame Napoleon retraced her steps and glanced out toward the vast Mediterranean Sea as she awaited her driver's return. Moments later she turned abruptly toward the car and rummaged through her purse to answer a persistently ringing phone.

"Kubri, here come some guards," announced Musa. "Should we turn around and drive off?"

"No, we are doing nothing wrong," said Kubri. "Let me handle this. Madame Napoleon's driver is trailing behind them. That's very odd."

Their own driver pulled out the engine's oil stick and examined it dramatically before wiping it clean. His hand was shaking slightly when he tried to push it back into place unhurriedly. All three men watched in surprise as Madame Napoleon's driver deserted the marching brigade and slunk back toward his car.

Soon the guards were upon them and demanding immediate answers in raised voices to hastily fired questions. Identification was mandatory. Thankfully all their papers were in order, but required a trip back to border headquarters for the senior looking guard to get legitimate confirmation.

When asked if they were planning to cross into Libya they were able to use the car "breakdown" as an excuse to turn back. Madame Napoleon glanced in their direction. None of them had ever met her in person so their identities were safe for now.

Long before the interrogation had ended, Madame's driver kicked up a cloud of dust and peeled out in front of them, speeding back down in the direction they'd come. Kubri and Musa looked at each other helplessly, yet still sure they had not been recognized. Perhaps in her role as detective she had noticed the constant presence of their car along the lonely coast road and wanted to challenge her suspicions officially. After an extended wait for the guards to return, they were released and flagged off with undue ceremony.

"Well I'm at least relieved that no major donkey ruse was uncovered," commented Kubri.

"Yes, no real harm done," added Musa. "I think our best hope now is to collect the Radcliffes and head south to Siwa.

"Full speed ahead."

-14-

Pursuit of the bishop

Dinner at the lodge that evening was relatively quiet considering the stimulating dynamic of being away on a family holiday. Both Baul parents seemed a bit distracted, although Rev. Baul skillfully kept the conversation flowing. After the family's rest period, there had been time for a hike up the Shali Lodge ruins with picturesque sunset photo opportunities at the top. They could see miles of dusty palm groves, blue-painted mud brick dwellings, the salt lake Birket Siwa, and beyond to the untainted sand sea waves seeming to lap at the edge of the oasis.

"I can't wait to try sand boarding tomorrow!" Joe exclaimed, refocusing the mood toward adventures ahead.

"Yeah, that sounds fun," said Miriam. "Grandpa, you could at least sled down a dune on a sand board. My friends at school said climbing back up in soft knee deep sand is the hardest part."

"We'll sleep well tomorrow night, that's for sure," observed Grandpa Baul before updating the rest of the family on the trio's plans for the following day. "I took the liberty of reserving a jeep and driver for most of the day. I'm sure he'll have sand boards too."

"I think I will probably stay around town and monitor the pigeon festival arrivals," announced Rev. Baul. "Things will be hopping by evening, I would guess. Hopefully Musa and Kubri will arrive during daylight hours."

"I knew you would be busy, darling, so I made arrangements for a full day of touring and perhaps exploring local charities, with a trusted local guide the hotel has arranged. They insist that I experience a Siwan sunrise," declared Mrs. Baul. "Is that okay with you?"

"Of course, my love," smiled Rev. Baul affectionately. "Anything you please. Would you like me to join you for the sunrise?"

"Oh don't bother," she replied. "You deserve to sleep in a bit. I won't be the only woman at the lodge signed up for such a day."

"I'm sure it's a popular offering," conceded Rev. Baul. "I would be honored to have you at my side for the beginning of the race on Saturday morning though."

"Absolutely, I wouldn't miss it," Mrs. Baul covered her relief with enthusiasm but then began to wonder why her protective husband had so readily agreed to let her venture off into unknown hazardous territory.

The whole family agreed the pigeon marathon was to be the high point of their trip. Grandpa took the opportunity to lay the groundwork for an earlier appearance than expected from Musa and Kubri, yet not revealing their current joint travel arrangements. Rev. Baul did not question the early arrival; he was very eager for them to join him.

As their ecolodge purposely had no electricity, a creative arrangement of palm oil candles and olive oil lanterns were set up all around so the family could enjoy a fun evening of card games before retiring to bed. Grandpa had wisely packed his own portable lightweight generator, which would continue to serve their electronic needs. He had upgraded the product months ago and it was now a clean and silent stable power source.

"Any news of Bishop Edwin?" Grandpa Baul privately asked his son after the others had said their goodnights. Their earlier search of his room that afternoon had yielded absolutely nothing.

"As a matter of fact I need to report something to Bishop Kareem but I have nothing new to tell him," explained Rev. Baul. "It's a real mystery. My visit to the small tourist information center this afternoon was useless. I would actually appreciate any help you can give me on that front, Dad. You always seem resourceful in uncertain circumstances."

"Actually I had an interesting conversation about the whole affair with Musa's friend, our hotel manager," disclosed Grandpa Baul. "He said the journalists that originally descended on his lodge left after almost no persistent investigative effort at all. He said they were all foreign bigwigs looking for a sensational story but didn't seem to know, or bother to ask, how the system really works in this part of the world."

"You mean about needing to gain trust with the right person before tongues will loosen?" queried Rev. Baul

"Exactly," replied Grandpa. "And this community doesn't even run like a mini-Cairo. They have a strong tribal family based mentality here, proud descendants of North

African Berbers, and even some ancient Greeks, for that matter. I bet you anything those hungry press mongers only talked to the local police force."

"What do you mean only the local police force?" asked Rev. Baul.

"They're just tourist police randomly assigned around the country to make foreigners feel safe, but they're not locals. They work under strict orders to stay out of Siwan affairs. The tribal leaders handle their informal justice system with the threat of facing councils, not jails," Grandpa Baul explained.

"What kind of punishment is imposed?"

"Being ostracized from the community is a peril worse than the death penalty in their minds. Very low crime rate here and not a jail to be found if you wanted one," Grandpa Baul pointed out.

"I see what you're saying," his son replied. "Even though we're searching for a tourist, no real progress will begin until the sheikhs get passionate about it. Human bureaucracy, people not paper."

"Right. I've established a good rapport with the manager here who has a generous spirit and is very astute," added Grandpa Baul. "Let me talk to him and see how he thinks we should proceed."

"Thank you," Rev. Baul looked more hopeful. "I feel responsible to Edwin's family to put things right. I can't imagine the agony they're going through now that the press is everywhere, with what so far have been erroneous leads."

"Is he married?" asked Grandpa Baul.

"No, but he's extremely close to his mother in London." said Rev. Baul. "She must be in a frantic state by now."

"I'll let you know something as soon as I do," assured his father. "The fact you know this bishop and his family personally will be an asset these journalists didn't have. Everyone here can relate to the bond of a father, son or brother. Let's connect in the morning."

"Sounds good," concluded Rev. Baul. "Sleep well, Dad."

"You too, son. We'll get to the bottom of this. I'm sure of it."

The anticipated knock came just after midnight; Madame Napoleon had arrived. Miriam quietly opened her door and let her brother inside. Grandpa was back at headquarters monitoring the talking bracelet, hoping she was wearing it after hours.

"The guy at the front desk just had a message sent to our room," confirmed Joe.

"Should we try to sneak a peek and make sure it's really Mom?" asked Miriam.

"Why not? She won't be coming to this wing because the other few rooms are reserved or full," pointed out Joe. "It definitely isn't the rest of our crew because of all the time they lost at the border fiasco and then having to pick up the Radcliffes."

Just as the kids stole around the corner of the hallway they spotted Grandpa flagging them down with a waving lantern. He confirmed the bracelet was silent except for some mild snoring intervals, so their mother was most likely in the lobby welcoming her friend.

"I wouldn't be surprised if your mother slipped something into your dad's after dinner drink to keep him sleeping soundly," proposed Grandpa.

"Poor Dad," said Joe.

"It's sure better than having him wake up and go searching for her," pointed out Miriam.

"True," said Grandpa. "Maybe I'm the least conspicuous one to be wandering anywhere near the lobby in the middle of the night. I don't know the night manager yet but obviously someone put in a good word for us or we wouldn't have been alerted."

Grandpa tiptoed down the hall wearing his favorite striped pajamas and was soon out of sight. Miriam and Joe slipped into Grandpa's room to wait. Less than ten minutes later he rapped on the door.

"It's Madame Napoleon alright," he exclaimed, a bit out of breath. "She looks a mess. I can't imagine she'll be in any shape for a sunrise camel trot. I've never seen such bloodshot eyes. You know they'll stick to their plan though, or else they may have to face our inquisitive company."

"How is Mom going to explain Madame Napoleon being here?" asked Joe.

"Maybe her husband needed her to represent the EU at a desert pigeon race?" Miriam suggested sarcastically.

They all laughed. No sense not going straight back to bed. Grandpa promised to welcome the rest of the gang when they arrived. It could still be hours unless the Radcliffe rendezvous had gone smoothly: lots of variables with buses and well-intentioned schedules. Grandpa was not pleased they had to drive unlit desert roads at night. The one down from the coast did have the luxury of asphalt, but that made speeds even higher and therefore more dangerous. Many drivers didn't even use headlights, adding to the number of head-on statistics each year.

"But Grandpa, Joe will get up when they come so I want to also," pleaded Miriam.

"Only on the condition you get back to bed right now and rest until you hear from me," Grandpa conceded. "Lady Sarah would probably come drag you out of bed anyway."

Before sending Miriam back to her room Grandpa Baul dialed Musa's phone for an update. The carload was relieved to hear Madame Napoleon had arrived safely. It would have put them in an awkward position if they'd found her car broken down as they drove by. Unfortunately they were still several hours away, but the Radcliffes were onboard. Sir Peter insisted on talking to Grandpa Baul before the conversation ended.

"Hello?" spoke a loud British accent.

"Sir Peter!" exclaimed Grandpa, nodding a smile toward his grandchildren.

"Hey, hey! What an adventure we are on this time," Sir Peter declared with great enthusiasm. "Our arrival anticipation has almost reached fever pitch."

"Thank you for coming to help us out," answered Grandpa generating a wide grin.

"We are delighted to be included in the mission," replied Sir Peter.

"We'll fill you in when you get here," said Grandpa. "I hope you've done a bit of dozing because you're going to hit the ground running."

"Brilliant! That's what I like to hear," he affirmed. "Brought all the supplies you requested."

"Super," said Grandpa. "See you soon."

"Okay. Over and out," shouted Sir Peter as he clicked off the connection.

Before heading back to sleep Grandpa Baul relayed the other end of the phone conversation. It would be hard for any of them to relax back into a state of slumber now.

Miriam borrowed a bottle of water from Grandpa and forced herself back down the hallway to her room.

"Miriam, shhh," came a voice the moment she unlocked her door.

"You scared me to death," cried Miriam as she lifted up her handheld light to see more clearly. "Mom! What are you doing here? How did you get in?"

"I'm so sorry dear," she apologized sincerely. "Where on earth have you been? I've been worried sick."

"I couldn't sleep," she stalled, glancing down at her water bottle. "I ran out of clean drinking water and Grandpa gave me some because I was so thirsty."

"Still you shouldn't be wandering hotel halls in the middle of the night," her mother reproached.

"What are you doing here? How did you get in?" she asked again.

"I'm sorry to have to involve you again, Miriam," she said. "But this is an emergency. Your father was given the extra key to your room as the front desk always distributes two copies. I couldn't risk being seen waiting outside your door."

"What's the matter?"

"Madame Napoleon is extremely feverish and clammy with a sore throat and headache. She needs some medicine quickly," she began.

"Madame Napoleon?"

"It's all too complicated to explain right now," she went on. "You'll just have to trust me and I'll explain it to you as soon as I'm am able. We must get her fever down before sunrise. I know that's not answering any of your questions, but do you have anything with you that would help? I packed in such a hurry it never crossed my mind."

"I don't have anything but I'm sure Grandpa does," she offered. "He won't mind if I wake him."

"Thank you so much, dear. I promise a full explanation as soon as possible. Not a word to your father, please. I am afraid his life is in danger as we speak," she added with a heightened sense of drama. "Madame Napoleon said two intimidating men were following her on her drive here. Imagine the fright: both terrorists most likely! We must not delay."

Miriam bit her lip. "I'll be right back, Mom."

-15-

The mysterious illness of Madame Napoleon

In the wee hours of Friday morning Joe appeared bleary eyed at Miriam's door once again. Miriam grabbed her key and rushed off down the hall behind him. Grandpa had just returned from checking in the new arrivals and the children eagerly welcomed them all.

"Joe, I can't believe how tall you've grown since our last visit," declared Sir Peter.

"I finally passed my sister," he pointed out.

Both Sir Peter and Lady Sarah had to tilt their warm smiles upward to meet the striking hazel eyes of their godson.

"Miriam your hair is beautiful, so long and thick," admired Lady Sarah.

"Thanks, I love your short stylish European haircut, Lady Sarah," said Miriam.

It was hard to know where to begin. The travelers assured Grandpa they had eaten a full meal before leaving the coast so would be fine until breakfast. All had rested well in the capable hands of their driver and would not hear of resting their heads until full details had been disclosed. The discussion was moved into the Radcliffes' accommodations next door to Grandpa and Joe's room. Grandpa had been lucky enough to secure them a spacious suite, the last private room at the end of the corridor.

The wrongly accused "terrorists" laughed contagiously at the news of Madame Napoleon's suspicions. Fortunately for them she must have kept the extent of her convictions to herself or they might not have left the border roundup at all. To assume Mrs. Baul was the only "loose cannon" in this tangle would be a severe underestimation of the situation at hand. Because members of the group would have to play multiple roles in just a few short hours, negotiations began as to who would serve each purpose most effectively. Sir Peter produced a well-worn notebook for the sorting out of details and discussion began in earnest.

Kubri was the only obvious choice for contacting the local sheikhs. Everyone saw this as crucial to all around success. He would accompany Rev. Baul, who would be a perfect representative of the Church at large. Musa would mastermind the electronic monitoring of events from hotel headquarters until he was needed at the pigeon loft, although Miriam promised to cover for him. He would not leave his surveillance post until all was cleared with the others.

"Musa," interrupted Sir Peter. "Do you remember the infamous felucca float you took us on from Cairo to Luxor to visit the pharaonic tombs?"

"How could I forget, Sir Peter?" smiled Musa.

"That was a voyage for the books," declared Lady Sarah gregariously. "We will forever trust you under any circumstances!"

"Sounds like a story we need to hear again once we are celebrating the finding of the Rt. Rev. and restoring peace to the region," declared Grandpa.

"Hear! Hear!" cheered Sir Peter.

Clearly Kubri had already been briefed on this Nile adventure as he smiled in recognition. Grandpa explained the status of plans brewing in the minds of their beloved Mrs. Baul and Madame Napoleon. Still hopefully harmless at this stage, their meddling could escalate out of control at a moment's notice. No one disagreed.

Several hours later Madame Napoleon's fever had not subsided. A frantic Mrs. Baul rapped repeatedly on her daughter's door.

"Miriam, wake up, it's your mother," she implored.

"What is it Mom?" Miriam asked as she stumbled over and opened her door.

"Madame Napoleon is very ill. I'm afraid she is in dire straits and I cannot possibly leave her unattended. Please, Miriam will you come to my rescue once again?" her mother begged.

"Why can't you sit with her?" asked Miriam.

"I must not delay with my camel trek, dear. I have to admit to you that my reasons have nothing to do with sightseeing but I can't say more without endangering our family's safety. I'm worried on all fronts as to what the future may hold."

"Calm down, Mom. Everything will be okay." Miriam tried in vain to convince her mother. Completely unsuccessful, Miriam finally accepted the keys to Madame

Napoleon's room and promised to engage a doctor if she didn't show signs of improvement.

"I know your father will fund a medical evacuation for Madame Napoleon back to Cairo if things come to that," assured her mother.

"Have you told him about what's going on?" probed Miriam.

"No, I was unable to rouse him with gentle shaking so thought it best to let things run their course. I promise to be back at the hotel by dinner if not before."

Miriam stood dumbfounded as the vague whirlwind explanation and engagement of her services took place. Just as her mother was slipping out of the room Miriam stooped down and caught an envelope that spilled out of her mother's bag. She started to call out and then stopped herself. They needed all the help they could get right now. Miriam turned the envelope over and held it closer to the lamp. Blank except for a long distance phone number written on the outside. She carefully unfolded the paper and read her mother's printed handwriting.

Press Release:

- Terrorist Cell Uncovered
- Weapons of Mass Destruction
- Kidnapped Bishop's Whereabouts Discovered

Thankfully still in draft form, the note was dangerous all the same. Miriam assumed the phone number on the envelope was for a fax machine. Knowing her mother and Madame Napoleon it was most likely destined for a western news agency. Trying to process the sudden start to her day,

Miriam splashed some cold water on her face before heading off to wake Grandpa and Joe.

"What?" yelled Joe, still tangled in his bed sheets.

"I'm telling you, Mom left her behind," Miriam explained.

"We better at least get Sir Peter up to take a look at Madame Napoleon," determined Grandpa. "It could just be a flu bug or a touch of food poisoning. You know how things can get exaggerated sometimes."

Both kids nodded in agreement. They would be able to monitor their mother's location and happenings from the lodge so it wasn't imperative that they pursue her yet. Grandpa would alert the others and suggest all meet together in half an hour. Miriam and Joe headed for their showers. A full day lay ahead.

"Sir Peter, are you awake?" Grandpa whispered loudly as he tapped on his neighbor's door.

"Coming! Just a moment," answered Lady Sarah with a sleepy yet still enthusiastic voice. She prodded her snoring husband awake.

"Grandpa Baul," exclaimed Sir Peter moments later as he sleepily opened the door. "Have we over slept? Please do come in."

"I'm so sorry to rouse you this early," Grandpa apologized, handing Sir Peter an already lit lantern. "Light is barely dawning outside but we're already in crisis."

As Grandpa explained the latest developments Sir Peter looked mildly concerned.

"Sarah and I will pop round with you to visit Madame Napoleon as soon as possible," announced Sir Peter. "The fever reducer will not have finished its course by now. She may just need some cool wet cloths and rest, but we'll do a full examination."

"Any suggestion as to a reason for our presence here?" asked Lady Sarah.

"I'm still working on that," answered Grandpa Baul. "I suppose Madame Napoleon really is the one whose presence needs explaining. We do need good reason though in order to convince my son."

"I propose we keep Musa and Kubri out of sight for now where Madame Napoleon is concerned," recommended Sir Peter. "No sense upsetting her further. If she's in a delusional state, seeing her feared terrorists might really push her over the edge."

Grandpa Baul couldn't help chuckle in the midst of the serious circumstances. He suggested they all get ready for the day and meet back shortly. If they didn't mind cramped quarters it might make most sense to meet in Grandpa Baul's room so they could include Musa in the conversation while he kept tabs on things electronically. Once the doctors had called on their patient they would be free to fine-tune the day's plans together. Grandpa Baul woke Musa and Kubri with a brief summary of the latest developments and then headed back to his own room.

"Hey Joe, I'm back," Grandpa called out as he unlocked their door.

"Miriam should be on her way back over here soon," said Joe. "The shower's free."

"Great. I'll shave and shower and then I want to check in on Madame Napoleon with your godparents before our meeting with everyone. Musa should be over shortly to help with monitoring. You could start getting the surveillance equipment hooked up again."

"Just what I was thinking."

"Madame Napoleon," called Miriam gently as she pushed the door open and held a flickering lantern in front of her.

"Who's there?" groaned a weak lethargic voice.

"It's Miriam Baul. My mother sent me to make sure you are okay," she explained. "I've brought along a friend of ours who is a doctor and wants to help you."

More groans. Lady Sarah sat herself down professionally on the edge of Madame Napoleon's bed. Miriam opened the curtains slightly to let in some natural light. No more complaints were uttered from the limp and suffering patient. Lady Sarah examined her throat, her ears and her eyes after finding her fever was still high. She took her blood pressure and listened carefully to her heart. Even Miriam could see she was having trouble breathing.

"Get me a damp cool cloth, please Miriam," asked Lady Sarah.

"Okay," Miriam found what she needed in the bathroom. "Is she going to be all right?"

"I'm not sure exactly what she's got," she explained. "She has a lot of different symptoms. Would you mind going and bringing Peter back for a second opinion?"

"Sure, I'll be right back."

Miriam found Sir Peter eager to be included in the patient's evaluation. He had assumed it would be an obvious diagnosis but if his wife were calling for him then something more serious was wrong. Moments later the doctor appeared at his wife's side and Lady Sarah listed what she had discovered before trading places with her husband.

Sir Peter's evaluation concurred with his wife's. Fever, sore throat, sore muscles, headache, chest pains and a raging eye infection: very odd combination.

"Sarah, this is reminding me of Jakarta," he stated hesitantly.

"That came to my mind as well," she agreed. "We're going to need blood tests run to be on the safe side."

"I'm sure there isn't a fully equipped lab here," Sir Peter pointed out. "Miriam, we're going to need to talk to her driver and see if we can get some questions answered about what she ate yesterday. Let's get your grandfather in here too and figure out what the next step is."

"I'll go get Grandpa," Miriam answered with a worried look on her face. As soon as Miriam closed the door the Radcliffes began a more aggressive line of questioning.

"Madame Napoleon," Peter called in a firm but gentle voice. "I need you to concentrate on what I'm saying. Stay with me. Have you been exposed to any poultry farms recently?" A slow but deliberate sideways shaking of her head accompanied by more miserable groaning confirmed that. "Have you eaten any raw eggs or chicken that was not cooked thoroughly?" A different reaction with an unsure muttering followed.

"Peter, I know Egypt has been on the list for the H5N1 strain of avian influenza but the only humans affected so far have been poultry workers," Lady Sarah explained. "I did read somewhere that they'd also detected the H7 strain, gift of a migrant bird found dead and wisely dissected. But still, the country has been very strict in its prevention of an outbreak and have sensibly stock piled the Tamiflu antiviral drug. I do think we are jumping to conclusions. It could be as simple as food poisoning."

"Sarah, you know as well as I do that we can't take any chances when we've got this combination of symptoms. The conjunctivitis could totally be a coincidence but I'm not convinced. Hopefully we'll get some more answers from her driver."

"I know you're right," agreed Sarah. "We won't regret erring on the side of caution, but the timing surely is unfortunate."

Grandpa Baul appeared at the door with Miriam. The Radcliffes filled them in on their diagnostic suspicions.

"Grandpa, Mom said that Dad could arrange for a medevac to Cairo if we needed it," explained Miriam. "I just thought she was being all dramatic at the time."

"We need to decide if we should bring your dad into the picture," said Grandpa Baul in all seriousness. "I could arrange the flight myself but the way things have escalated I am inclined to think we need to have him on our side, and not only to pick up the bill. What good is it doing sheltering him from his wife's actions at this point?"

"Why don't we decide at our meeting with everyone?" suggested Lady Sarah.

"Yes, good thinking," replied Grandpa. "There is a lot at stake here. Let's talk elsewhere at any rate. Is she okay to rest a bit on her own?"

"I'll keep checking in on her but we need to secure a medevac aero team immediately," Sir Peter announced.

"With all the chartered planes coming in for the race it shouldn't be a problem at all," replied Grandpa. "The race. If this leaks to the press, a possible bird flu case, we're done for."

"I don't recommend alerting anyone as to the full extent of our suspicions right now," said Sir Peter. "Not even her husband needs these details until we know something conclusive. It would be wrong to panic anyone and we don't have evidence to necessitate shutting down a bird race. Just the diagnosis of hospitalization needed should be grounds enough to request emergency medical assistance. As we said, it could be as simple as food poisoning."

"I agree," confirmed Grandpa Baul. "I will go speak to the front desk and get the ball rolling but I'll need my son to sign off on the bill. You go talk with the others and I'll meet you there soon."

-16-

The stalking journalist

The group formed more plans following an all too brief night's rest. With the new developments, adjustments had to be made. The issues at hand were diverse and complicated. All agreed to work as a team, voting Grandpa Baul in as operations lead. They needed to depend on their well-laid plans while remaining flexible enough to pursue backup options.

Unanimously they decided to take Rev. Baul into their confidence over breakfast. There appeared to be no other way forward and his resources and experience would be needed in the hours ahead. But the group chose to keep secret the extent of their electronic reconnaissance resources and the grandiose imagination of Rev. Baul's lovely wife. Some expressed reservations as to his full cooperation if all were revealed. To serve their overall intent not to harm in the process of procuring peace, Rev. Baul would not only need to see the importance of his role in rescuing the missing bishop but also in protecting his wife from impending danger.

Before the prearranged breakfast rendezvous, Grandpa Baul knocked on his son's door to brief him on the presence of Madame Napoleon and her dire need for medevac services. With surprisingly few questions Rev. Baul readily agreed to make it possible. Grandpa Baul kept the identity of the able foreign doctors helping Madame Napoleon to himself for the moment, still unsure quite how to explain their presence. Eager to be a part of the action, his son offered to make all the arrangements with the hotel manager's assistance. He would join them at the rooftop restaurant for breakfast as soon as the details were settled.

Mango drinks, pomegranates and freshly picked dates arrived as the guests found their places. An appetizing menu listed items in both Arabic and English: fresh yogurt, eggs, local bread and thick date syrup. The guests all took time to enjoy the spectacular view from the restaurant. Nestled into the foot of an impressive white salt rock mountain along the end of the salt lake, they could see olive groves, palm groves, and endless miles of rolling sand. Resembling an ancient Berber village, their ecolodge blended perfectly into its natural surroundings. Built like traditional Siwan kershel houses, using sun dried salt rock mixed with straw, helped create a natural atmosphere of desert-style comfort.

Rev. Baul eventually arrived on the rooftop, still looking slightly groggy from the interruption to his deep night's sleep. After getting his bearings he looked around in astonishment as he recognized his waiting friends.

"Sir Peter and Lady Sarah!" he declared. "I am speechless."

"So good to see you," announced Sir Peter as the two doctors rose enthusiastically and gave their friend warm embraces.

"What has brought you two here?" asked Rev. Baul.

"You know us," started Sir Peter.

"Full of surprises we are," added Lady Sarah. "Got news from our godson that you were racing some birds in an exotic location."

"How could we resist?" asked Sir Peter.

"Well I am delighted beyond words," said Rev. Baul. "Kubri, Musa! You're here already too?"

"My business resolved itself more quickly than I expected," said Kubri. "I was glad to be able to get here as soon as possible."

"Wonderful," Rev. Baul shook his hand eagerly.

"Plans with my cousins fell through so I drove straight on," explained Musa. "Didn't want to miss anything important on this end."

"I'm really happy to see you all here," said Rev. Baul taking a seat and looking around as if someone were missing. "Oh, my adventuresome wife sauntered off at sunrise for a full day of touring. I'm so sorry she is missing this great event. But she'll be thrilled to find you here later."

"We look forward to seeing her," affirmed Lady Sarah.

"You two aren't the foreign mystery physicians I've been hearing about are you?" asked Rev. Baul suddenly seeing the full picture more clearly.

"At your service," Sir Peter answered with an impromptu bow from his seat.

"You certainly have been working overtime," Rev. Baul said with much admiration in his voice.

"We are just so pleased to be here," Lady Sarah clarified. "Too soon to know the outcome of Madame Napoleon's illness but thank you very much for arranging proper emergency assistance."

"It's the least I can do," confirmed Rev. Baul. "This is my wife's dearest friend here in Egypt. She will be in quite a state of shock to find her friend whisked off across the country to the hospital."

"No need to worry about that," encouraged Sir Peter. "Knowing your wife, she will rise to the occasion and just be grateful she is in good hands."

"True," Rev. Baul concluded. "Your confirmation will reassure her. You know how worked up she can get sometimes."

All present smiled knowingly and the subject was tactfully changed to a different topic of mutual interest.

Eating breakfast at a table on the opposite side of the ecolodge rooftop that morning was a man who looked very out of place in such a setting. His back was toward them but it was still quite obvious that he was dressed flawlessly in desert oasis attire wearing a spotless white shirt, unwrinkled khaki pants and a hat that showed no signs of sun exposure. Grandpa discreetly pointed out his presence as breakfast drew to a close and voices had risen well past a minimal volume.

"I saw him check in last night before I went to bed," noted Rev. Baul quietly. "Struck up a conversation in fact. He said he was a journalist from the Associated Foreign Press, if I remember correctly."

"That's odd, he sure looks familiar," mused Kubri.

"Since all the other journalists seem to have fled the region, did he say why he is here?" asked Musa.

"Yes. He came to report the Siwa-Cairo pigeon race proceedings on behalf of interested fanciers in Europe," explained Rev. Baul. "He said there is quite a following on the continent with Belgium at the epicenter."

"I'd say he seems a bit preoccupied with the other guest sharing his table this morning," noted Kubri.

Everyone stole discrete glances in the direction of the reporter, only to see the back of his head focused with great concentration on the presence of a European blond.

"Probably his wife," commented Rev. Baul.

"Or an important business associate," added Sir Peter with a wink after glancing at their empty ring fingers.

"Really now boys," Lady Sarah stepped in. Miriam broke the tension with a loud burst of laughter and the couple briefly turned their heads in their direction.

"Fine. I hate to interrupt this productive meeting but I had better go make another room call on our dear Madame Napoleon," announced Sir Peter. "We can't afford to have the medevac team find her in any worse shape than she already is. Thankfully she seemed to have slipped into a more peaceful sleep after the injection you gave her, Sarah."

"The plane should be landing within the hour," said Rev. Baul after consulting his watch. "I was able to get ahold of Monsieur Napoleon's assistant at the EU headquarters in Cairo and she assured me he would be pulled out of meetings in Brussels and told immediately about his wife's situation. The control tower has a slight concern about the weather here though. Apparently an unexpected sandstorm is brewing. Landing in Siwa won't be a problem for the aircraft but if the wind direction doesn't cooperate then taking off immediately may be a problem."

"Let's hope for the best. Who will meet the flight in Cairo?" asked Lady Sarah.

"His assistant agreed to meet the airplane herself and stay with Madame Napoleon until her husband can get a flight back," Rev. Baul explained. "The mission will hire a private nurse to stay with her as long as she's in the hospital. I promised we would check in with her as soon as we arrived back. She has my satellite number to notify us of any further developments. My wife will be horrified to learn of the seriousness of her friend's sickness. What a terrible shame she cannot be present to offer her support."

"Maybe it's better in the long run," suggested Grandpa Baul. "She would probably be unduly upset by the whole thing. Thanks to the Radcliffes all precautions have been taken to ensure a full recovery is possible."

"Yes, thank you again," said Rev. Baul warmly.

"I'd better get back to business myself," announced Musa. "Delicious breakfast in an exotic desert oasis. I could get used to this."

"Me too. I'll come with you, Musa," offered Joe.

"Please do," Musa eagerly accepted.

"Miriam, why don't we go peek in on Madame Napoleon too," suggested Lady Sarah.

"Okay. I'll find you later, Joe," said Miriam. "Thanks for breakfast, Dad."

"My pleasure. All fresh food from the earth, it doesn't get better than that," Rev. Baul reflected appreciatively.

Everyone disappeared from the table except Rev. Baul and Kubri. Taking a moment to admire the craftsmanship of their palm trunk table and woven palm frond chairs, Rev. Baul returned to matters at hand. They each asked for coffee refills and relaxed, fortifying them for the full day ahead.

"I'm going to head into the town center and see if I can organize a meeting with the head of Siwa's judicial council," explained Kubri.

"How can I help on that front?" asked Rev. Baul.

"Let me see if I can get things arranged adequately and then I propose you join me for the meeting to represent officially Bishop Kareem in Cairo.

"That sounds like an excellent plan," confirmed Rev. Baul. "Let's stay in touch by phone."

"Why don't we check in on your mom, Joe?" suggested Musa.

"Last seen wandering the desert aimlessly on camelback," Joe teased.

"Good to see your sense of humor is still sharp," noted Grandpa Baul as he secured the door to their temporary headquarters.

"Joe, can you activate the GPS locator linked to your mom's satellite phone?" asked Musa. "I'll fine-tune the bracelet receptor."

"Miriam told me she checked for it on your mother's wrist after she'd gotten dressed this morning; she was wearing it," confirmed Grandpa.

"Perfect," added Musa.

"Did anyone ever get a hold of Madame Napoleon's driver?" asked Joe out of curiosity.

"Yes, actually he was being housed with the other out of town drivers down the road," explained Grandpa. "Kubri handled that with our lodge manager. Apparently he was pretty shaken up about being pulled out of bed so early, especially in front of the other sleeping guests."

"Did he have any useful information to contribute?" queried Musa.

"No, they had eaten separately," answered Grandpa. "I'm thankful we've taken the medevac route. She'll be well cared for in Cairo."

"Grandpa, can you please hand me that map of the area?" Joe pointed out his request.

"Sure, here you go."

"Looks like they haven't even gotten off the beaten trail yet," said Joe pointing to a spot on the map so the others could see.

"Camels are reliable creatures," said Musa. "But they're not sprinters, especially with people onboard and trudging through the kind of sand they have around here."

"I'd like to know who else is with them," commented Grandpa Baul. "The lodge manager should at least be able to give us a viable head count. I doubt they've got a far off destination planned, but it would be nice to know where they're heading."

"Mom sure is going to be hobbling around tonight if she stays on a camel all day," added Joe. "What was she thinking?"

They all smiled empathetically at such an image before being interrupted by a coded knock on the door.

"Miriam, come in," Grandpa pulled the door open and let her inside.

"Dad said he's going to the airstrip soon and Sir Peter and Lady Sarah have worked out a makeshift stretcher for Madame Napoleon."

"Did you hear him mention anything about a meeting with Kubri and the local sheikhs?" queried Grandpa Baul.

"Yeah, the hotel manager said it was way too early to make a call unless it was an emergency," explained Miriam. "Kubri told him it was exactly that. While Dad is gone,

Kubri is going to go in to the village headquarters to request a meeting face to face."

"Good thinking," commented Grandpa. "We're fortunate to have Kubri with us in all this."

"Yeah, I really like him," said Miriam.

"Me too," added Joe.

"What are the chances I would have ended up giving Kubri a ride to Siwa?" asked Musa. "We've been so busy I haven't told you the whole story. Sir Peter and Lady Sarah thought I was making it all up at first."

"Speaking of Sir Peter," said Grandpa. "Does anyone know if he's had a chance to get his hands on some appropriate disguises?"

"That was next on his list when I left him," confirmed Miriam.

"Mister Baul," came an accented voice from the hallway, accompanied by an unrecognized rhythm on the door.

"Yes, coming," Grandpa Baul responded as he motioned Musa and his grandkids to block full view of their surveillance equipment. Opening his door, Grandpa stepped out into the hallway leaving his door slightly ajar.

"There is a gentleman in the front lobby asking to speak to the elder of your party," explained the young man sent to retrieve him.

"I can come with you right now," offered Grandpa Baul.

"I wonder who is asking after Grandpa?" said Miriam.

"Let's go find out," suggested Joe.

"Go ahead you two," said Musa. "Just stay invisible."

"No problem," said Joe as he and his sister peered down the hallway in the direction Grandpa had gone.

Moments later they screeched to a halt before entering the lobby.

"That's the man from the other breakfast table," whispered Joe as he pulled his sister behind the cover of some potted papyrus plants.

"He better not have been eavesdropping on us at breakfast," warned Miriam.

"Oh, oh. I think he's snooping around for a scoop on the medevac patient," said Joe as he watched the reporter's tall frame straighten eagerly when Rev. Baul appeared in the lobby to hire several porters to help carry the stretcher.

"Better to have him curious about that then the rest of our conversation," said Miriam.

"Good point," Joe whispered back.

Grandpa Baul astutely pulled the journalist off to the side in an effort to divert him from interrogating his son. All they could see was Grandpa's head nodding up and down. The reporter had a look of mild disappointment on his face but he didn't appear to be the type to give up quite so easily.

"We'd better warn Sir Peter that they might get hassled by the press," said Joe before running off to find the Radcliffes.

"I'll stay here and see if I'm needed," said Miriam. "They must be in Madame Napoleon's room. You'd better hurry."

"Yes, the Radcliffes," Miriam heard her grandfather's voice rise in aggravation. "You overheard correctly. Sir Peter and Lady Sarah, the renowned British physicians in the region."

Grandpa Baul intentionally shifted positions so Miriam could now see his face. She couldn't hear the questions being asked but from her vantage point she was definitely able to hear the answers. Obviously Grandpa was making a point of projecting in her direction. Clearly their love struck breakfast companion had ears they hadn't anticipated this morning. But replaying the rooftop conversation through in her mind, she realized they had already been wording things carefully because of the presence of her father.

"No, I can't promise you that," said Grandpa Baul kindly but firmly. "They are here on vacation to enjoy the race festivities."

The man stood to attention excitedly when he heard commotion coming from the guest rooms behind Miriam. Miriam joined the entourage and entered the lobby at the head of the medical procession. Grandpa gave her a look of thanks as she apologetically nudged the journalist to the side to make way for the stretcher to pass through the front doors of the lodge. Madame Napoleon certainly looked very sick but seemed to be holding her own. Help was on the way. Miriam and Grandpa waved goodbye as the car drove off to the airport; the journalist was left behind flailing his arms desperately in an attempt to flag down a nonexistent taxi.

"Where are they when you need them?" muttered the reporter as he briskly brushed past them and reentered the lobby. "I'm not done with you yet, Mr. Baul," he called back over his shoulder.

"That sounds a bit threatening," said Miriam.

"I think we'd better move out," Grandpa suggested. "He must be under a lot of pressure to produce something news worthy. A desert bird race is hardly a big seller."

-17-

Camels and pigeons

Not twenty minutes into the sunrise jaunt Mrs. Baul was wiping sweat from her forehead where her sunhat was squeezing too tightly. They had been driven from the ecolodge to the edge of the Siwa Oasis and picked up their camel caravan at the point where the road met pure sand. Their leader warned them that a bit of blowing sand was to be expected for the day but nothing severe; this was not *Khamseen* season when swirling sandstorms dumped relentlessly on Egypt and beyond.

Mrs. Baul's camel was friendly enough but hardly produced a calming rhythm. Thankfully she was not wearing a skirt so could follow her guide's instructions and attempt to rest her feet up on her camel's lengthy strong neck. This was a traditional Tuareg custom from the other side of the Sahara Desert, he explained, but something camels respected because it let them know who was in control. However, the next shouted command that she relax back into the saddle seemed futile.

The sky was not as light as she would have expected once the sun fully filled the atmosphere. A hot breeze was kicking up sand and started to bother Mrs. Baul's eyes even behind the protection of her sunglasses. She looked at the small group she was traveling with and hoped their first planned rest stop would soon appear. Fresh water springs would be a welcomed sight and hopefully provide a natural opportunity to interview the caravan leader.

Mrs. Baul was already regretting her decision to leave Madame Napoleon behind, but under the pressing circumstances she did not feel she had any choice in the matter. She was sure her friend would have done the same if roles had been reversed. The situation was now escalating beyond either of their control. She must discipline herself to keep all anxiety in check. Before her friend had arrived and collapsed in exhaustion, she had called Mrs. Baul at several points along her road journey down from the coast. The sighting of terrorists on their trail was shocking. Both assumed they were up against large forces, but neither had truly expected such a turn of events. They were supposed to be the ones stalking evil schemes toward international exposure. Instead they were the hunted.

Worried thoughts swirled around in Mrs. Baul's mind. The last coherent update she had received from Madame Napoleon had been gathered covertly from her supposed EU informant. The kidnapped bishop incident had finally reached the eyes of international leaders, although they often insisted on the word "missing" rather than "kidnapped." Deep cover agents would soon be descending upon Egypt. No longer was this a story just for the feeding of hungry journalists. The outcome was threatening and Madame Napoleon had communicated her fears that these investigative agencies had no inkling as to what was at stake. None seemed to realize the link to weapons of mass destruction or even terrorist cells. It had become their personal duties in the light of such information at their disposal to act swiftly, before more lives were endangered.

Mrs. Baul regained her composure and steeled herself with these convictions against what lay ahead. Because nothing had been found at the Donkey Rescue in Siwa proper, both women had agreed the next plan of attack would be to embed themselves with desert experts. Who better than an experienced camel guide? Although the journalists had gotten impatient and gone elsewhere, Madame Napoleon assured her friend that the undercover emissaries en route to Egypt were heading directly to the Siwa Oasis.

Rev. Baul and the Radcliffes returned from seeing the medical evacuee safely on her way and agreed to meet up with each other later in the day. Thankfully the winds had cooperated and the airplane took off again without incident.

"I desperately want to check in on my racing pigeons," announced Rev. Baul, "But I don't want to put you two through the sludge of bird lofts and the jostling of contestants until I've seen the full setup this morning."

"No problem at all," said Lady Sarah. "Why don't we rest at the lodge for a while, darling?"

"Brilliant," added Peter. "We can slip out for a bit of sightseeing once we're feeling more rested."

"I would like our whole party to be together for dinner this evening with the welcome addition of my wife's presence," reminded Rev. Baul.

"Splendid," confirmed Lady Sarah. "There will be plenty of time to catch up together later. I know your wife would be terribly offended if she missed as much as a single conversation."

"You're quite right there," agreed Rev. Baul happily. "No sense repeating ourselves."

Rev. Baul headed off in pursuit of pigeon headquarters as he waited to hear if Kubri had made any progress with the local leaders. It was ashamedly a relief to Rev. Baul that his wife was gone for the day, as she was sure to interpret his constant presence at the pigeon lofts as a relapse into an obsession he had long ago convinced her was ungrounded. The Radcliffes did some impromptu bird watching around the extensive lodge property before returning to the command center for an update from Musa and Grandpa Baul on the status of their beloved Mrs. Baul.

"Musa, is that you?" Rev. Baul sounded panicked on the other end of the line.

"Rev. Baul?" guessed Musa.

"Musa, I just got to the pigeon loft and one of our birds is missing! My prize pigeon is gone!" shouted Rev. Baul, clearly in competition with a noisy market activity.

"What?" Musa was stunned. "Rev. Baul says one of our pigeons is missing," Musa repeated to the rest of the room.

"Missing?" asked Grandpa Baul. "Does he think it's been stolen?

"Which pigeon?" asked Miriam distressed.

"Which bird is missing? Do you think someone stole it, or maybe the cage was left open by mistake?" suggested Musa.

"No. Definitely not a mistake or its mate would have flown off too," explained Rev. Baul. "It was the large male."

"Cinnamon," Musa announced to the others.

"Cinnamon?" moaned Miriam.

"You should see the quality of other birds here," continued Rev. Baul. "He was the best-bred one! None of the Swifts have any sign of show bird in them. They're overfed and missing feathers."

"Maybe their only concern is speed," suggested Musa.

"You may be right," he added. "It's possible they race well but it looks like sloppy breeding to me."

"Wow. I am so sorry. Aren't there any guards around?" asked Musa.

"Yes, lots of them. All the police have the tourist/antiquities sign wrapped around their arms. The race coordinator said they are not allowing owners to do any bird tosses whatsoever, despite the many complaints that their feathered athletes need some exercise. They aren't even letting birds wander past their perches into the open aviaries because of the looming sandstorm."

"But why wouldn't they have stolen the pair?" queried Musa.

"Oh, I can't believe this," moaned Rev. Baul.

"What do we do now?" queried Musa.

"Son, do you want us to come down there right away?" Grandpa Baul had asked for the phone from Musa.

"Yes, I guess so," replied Rev. Baul. "No, I don't know. Maybe I need to try to track down the night manager or the late shift of guards to see if there were any unknown people hanging around."

"Do you think it could have been a jealous contestant trying to sabotage the race?" asked Grandpa.

"I have no idea. I'll ask around and see if anyone else is missing birds," said Rev. Baul, now sounding calmer and regaining his quick reasoning. "Don't bother coming down right now, Dad. I'll call you back once I find out more."

"Okay. Don't worry we'll find him," assured Grandpa Baul. "He won't be happy to be separated from his partner for long."

"You are right about that," agreed Rev. Baul. "I suppose if he isn't being held against his will he should return within the day, unless he's confused, false starts the race and heads for home."

"One step at a time, son. Call us once you know more," said Grandpa.

"Thanks Dad, I'll talk to you soon. Goodbye."

"Bye," said Grandpa and then hung up the phone. "What do you think about this new development?"

"Poor Cinnamon, poor Sugar," groaned Miriam.

"Coincidence or not?" Sir Peter mused.

"I think we've been working in Gaza too long to be objective anymore," pointed out Lady Sarah.

"Possibly," agreed Sir Peter.

"I'm sure you could tell us stories," added Grandpa Baul.

"We surely could. Some we can't even bring ourselves to repeat to each other," said Lady Sarah truthfully.

"Wow. That sure puts things in perspective quickly," said Grandpa. "And I'm sure you're not talking about kidnapped pigeon tragedies."

"But what on earth could a missing pigeon have to do with the other conspiracy theories we're trying so hard to put a stop to?" asked Joe logically.

"Yeah, there's no way this can relate to the missing bishop," said Miriam. "Maybe that journalist guy is holding a grudge and it was the only way he could think of to get revenge on us?"

"You've been reading too many fiction novels, young lady," Lady Sarah lightened the atmosphere with an infectious laugh. There was not much more that could be done but wait.

"Mom wouldn't have done anything like that would she?" asked Joe.

"It wouldn't make any sense if she had," said Grandpa. "What would her motive be? She's trying to protect, not hurt your father."

"No, it can't have anything to do with her," decided Joe.

"Joe, we've never tried it out in an uncontrolled setting but the microscopic electronic dot we put on that pigeon's beak might be just what we need to sort this out," said Musa.

"I hadn't thought of that," replied Joe. "Does Dad know about it?"

"Not yet. I didn't want him to know I'm experimenting with his prize racers," grinned Musa guiltily.

Musa elaborated the theory behind the experimental device. Grandpa had only been briefed on it during the initial brainstorming phase.

"Nothing this small is on the market yet," Musa explained. "Usually such things are attached to a pigeon post on the bird's leg. But that is way too obvious for discrete heat sensitive search and rescue operations where a flyer risks capture."

"Sounds to me like this scientific hobby, as you call it, is keeping your bright mind challenged," noted Grandpa admiringly. "You kids are definitely getting a far-reaching education outside the walls of your school."

"I'd take this kind of learning any day," announced Joe.

"Me too!" agreed Miriam.

"Both pigeons already had this magnetic gadget embedded in their beaks," Musa elaborated. "But I think they may still be a bit too young to have perfected their homing instincts without some long distance racing experience under their wings, so to speak."

Kubri found himself drowning in a bureaucratic tangle; one office to the next and back again. His patience quota for the day had been depleted within several short minutes of game playing, but he persevered. It wasn't until he sat down exhausted with a glass of mint tea that he began to understand the workings of the town. Foreigners, whether western or non-Siwan Egyptian, were doomed to failure without an empathetic respect for the culture: he impatiently searched his mind for a new approach.

As he looked out over the center town square, he smiled as he watched children dashing around pushing each other in old wooden wheelbarrows and squealing with happiness when one tipped over. An older gentleman asked Kubri in perfect Arabic if he could join him at his table. One topic led to another and Kubri was welcomed into the wise man's confidence as only an honored guest might expect. The aged man wore a long spotless white *galabeya* and had an immaculately trimmed graying beard. His welcoming dark brown eyes stood out beneath striking deep brown lines etched into his brow.

Slowly Kubri's questions were answered honestly and amiably and the next thing he knew the elderly man, Haj Sayed, was insisting that Kubri and his traveling companions honor him in his home for a meal.

"That's a very generous offer, Haj Sayed," said Kubri. "I am pleased to accept your invitation on behalf of my friends."

"Thank you, I am honored," Haj Sayed nodded respectfully.

"Haj Sayed, do you know any of the Siwan head sheikhs personally?"

"Of course everyone in this oasis is related somehow, as the large number of albinos confirms," he explained. "My cousin is chief of one of the eleven tribes of Siwa but he is off on the annual initiation ceremony with all boys who were coming of age."

"That sounds like an interesting rite of passage," noted Kubri.

"Very. It takes place every year in the desert at a cold spring not far from the edge of the oasis. It's a wonderful time for young men to bond with their fathers and brothers across tribes."

"How long do they go off for?"

"Weeks. I'm not sure exactly," Haj Sayed admitted. "Isolation in a desert setting serves to increase the youths' respect for their elders and they learn new skills of survival. It is certain to unite them in trust, and to test their inner strength."

"Haj Sayed, I have a friend who is here visiting your beautiful oasis and has lost someone dear to his heart," explained Kubri.

"This is a very hard thing to bear," replied the old man. "Please tell me how it happened."

"We don't really know exactly," said Kubri. "My friend is a guest to your haven here and would like to ask to be put under the protection of your care."

"This I cannot refuse," Haj Sayed's eyes slowly wandered upward as he reflected on the expansive canopy of sky. "What you ask must be honored."

"The word of your traditions is true then," said Kubri in a serious frame of mind. "My father is a chief far off on the other side of the Great River. He has passed down wise stories of your people to ours."

"Then we are brothers," confirmed the man in a gentle tone of voice, his smile deepening his brown wrinkles. "I passed through your land on pilgrimage once. Many years ago that was. I had studied as a young man at the great Al-Azhar Mosque in Cairo and then sought my fortune in far off fields. Eventually my heart turned back toward home."

"And so you bear the title, *Haj*, pilgrim. You have been blessed," Kubri sensed this man's profound spirit.

"Thank you, my friend," answered Haj Sayed. "Now, to matters at hand."

Back at lodge headquarters Sir Peter and Lady Sarah were awaiting instructions from the tech team before being deployed to their prearranged position. The GPS device was still tracking Mrs. Baul's every move and the bracelet efficiently monitoring any audible conversation. All ears paid attention when they heard her caravan leader command them to halt and dismount.

"Now, ladies and gentlemen," he shouted with a mock English accent. "There are more of you on our ride than I'd expected this morning. I must go on ahead without you past the next sand sea dune to see if the hot springs are free for our group. I will return shortly. Rest while you can."

"Where is he going?" Mrs. Baul's voice boomed in and out.

"Said he'd be right back," came another woman's voice: an Australian tourist perhaps.

"I sure hope he isn't deserting us," said Mrs. Baul, imagining a variety of wary scenarios. "He promised us we would get to the spring by noon and if I'm not mistaken the sun is almost straight up above us now."

"Don't worry," said a young man's gruff voice. "Leaving us high and dry isn't going to buy him his dinner."

"Have either of you heard any local rumblings about the kidnapped bishop?" asked Mrs. Baul bravely.

"What bishop?" asked the woman.

"You know, the one that was in the news earlier this week," said the man.

"Oh, that was in Libya wasn't it?" she asked.

"Actually the press thought so at first, then they followed a lead to Siwa but found nothing," explained Mrs. Baul.

"So where is he?" asked the man.

"That is exactly what I'm trying to find out," answered Mrs. Baul.

"You're not some deep cover agent, are you?" the woman's voice sounded a bit put off.

"Not exactly, just keeping my eyes and ears open," Mrs. Baul replied with unnecessary defense in her voice, hoping her tenuous courage would hold out.

"We're not accusing you of anything lady," said the man. "We want adventure as much as anyone but we're not going to go sticking our foreign noses in places we don't belong. My legs are killing me."

"Just walk it off honey," the woman yelled, sounding much fainter than before.

"Grandpa, why would the guy leave his own caravan?" asked Miriam.

"I'm not sure," he replied. "It sounds like there are a lot of riders though according to what the caravan leader said. But there sure aren't many voices in the background. By the way, the front desk confirmed the tour would bypass the hot springs this time of year because the sulfur levels are too high and the mosquitoes are rampant."

"That's odd," said Joe. "So why are they stopped near them? Do we need to head out for some sand boarding?"

"Soon Joe, I promise," answered Grandpa. "We need to have a few more pieces of the puzzle in place before we reposition ourselves."

-18-

Magnoon Abdu

With no new developments at the pigeon lofts, Rev. Baul took some time to think through his sermon that he had been pondering all week. Pentecost Day, fifty days after Easter, was his favorite service of the year, due solely to the fact that he got to release a white dove in the church garden, symbolic of the Holy Spirit's presence in the world. Admittedly the first year had been a disaster when he'd used a real dove. He had been unable to purchase a pure white dove locally so he enthusiastically embraced the challenge of breeding one for the occasion. His dear wife did not see the necessity of countless hours spent among his feathered friends and declared the project an unhealthy addiction of sorts.

Yet when the day of celebration finally arrived she was as enthusiastic as the rest of the congregation. Immediately following the recessional hymn the congregation moved into the church garden and the children had gathered round Rev. Baul taking turns touching the bird's silky white feathers in the final moments of its captivity. After the recitation of a short litany Rev. Baul dramatically tossed the dove high into the air. Thankfully the children had moved on to dashing about the garden before a nearby hawk consumed that ancient church symbol. From that experience on they used hardy white homing pigeons.

Mrs. Baul soon grew anxious at the disappearance of her caravan leader and decided to leave her camel chewing its cud and see if she could peer over the sand dune in front of them without attracting attention. She wandered off as nonchalantly as possible under the pretense of wanting a more picturesque view. Climbing to the top of the sandy mound proved to be much more difficult than these camels let on. Trudging along in the sand Mrs. Baul was reminded of her first attempt at snowshoeing on their honeymoon years ago. She glanced back at her contented camel and realized the design of his wide spread hooves would act as a perfect sandshoe.

Thinking about those special memories made her worry about her husband yet again and the possible danger closing in on them all. Her primary concern was that he did not seem aware of the risks he was taking in pursuing his friendship with Kubri. It would devastate him when true identities were exposed. Should she have warned him at their lunch when the opportunity had arisen? It was against her better judgment to remain silent, but her husband had emphasized the need for concrete facts. He may have been right but facts were quickly coming together, as developments of the week were proving. On the other hand, since he was the professional, perhaps this was a well-concealed cover even from his own wife, giving him free reign to probe the Middle Eastern underworld. Only time would tell. Fresh bursts of blowing sand swirled about as Mrs. Baul tucked her scarf securely around her face and pushed forward.

Less than half way up the ridge Mrs. Baul heard a yell from below. She turned around to find the tourist couple she had been riding next to shouting at the top of their lungs. Waving her camera and pointing upward they seemed to understand her signals. After all, she was hardly going to get far on her aching legs without a camel securely beneath her. Eventually the top of the dune greeted her with success and she searched for the caravan leader. She froze in panic at what met her eyes: barren waves of sand, one after another, after another, after another. Under different circumstances she could have reveled for hours in the beauty of such a meditative landscape. The faint outline of hoof prints pointed in the direction of their leader's disappearance.

Mrs. Baul called down urgently to the rest of her party. Throwing her arms up in the air she tried to convince them their leader was gone. Her heavy breathing and yelling, being heard back at the lodge through her electronic monitoring device, aroused the attention of the lodge headquarters' operators. Unfortunately the only clear sounds coming through on the monitoring instrument were her last shouts, the rest of her distressed communications were pantomimed shadows.

"What is going on?" Joe asked suddenly.

"Is she in trouble?" asked Miriam.

"We really could use a visual feed on the scene," bemoaned Musa.

"Should we get into our gear then, Grandpa Baul?" queried Sir Peter.

"Yes, I think the time has come," answered Grandpa.

Both Sir Peter and Lady Sarah could hardly disguise their delight at the pronouncement. Watches were synchronized and phone batteries double-checked. Musa ceremonially handed Sir Peter a gift before he left.

"Prayer beads, thank you Musa," said Sir Peter.

"You'll need them Sir Peter, if you know what I mean."

"Oh, I see," Sir Peter raised his eyebrows melodramatically. "Sarah darling, we'll have to watch what we say now. It looks like big ears will be tuning in."

Lady Sarah ignored her husband's attempt at a witty remark and turned toward the others. "We will be with you all in spirit," she announced as they prepared to depart.

"Grandpa can we go yet?" asked Joe.

"Musa, what do you think?" queried Grandpa Baul.

"Please!" Miriam joined in.

"Let me contact your driver and see what he thinks about the threatening sandstorm," said Musa. "He knows the ways of the desert better than I do."

"Do you think we really will get to do some sand boarding?" asked Joe, his concern for his mother not dominating his thoughts at that moment.

"We'll make sure you get some in when all this blows over," said Musa. "I'll let him know it's on your agenda. The only unknown variable is the brewing storm."

"How are we going to find Mom?" asked Miriam.

"Grandpa Baul, you did make sure he has GPS in his jeep right?" queried Musa.

"Hello, Musa?" Rev. Baul was on the line again.

"Yes, Rev. Baul!" said Musa. "We've been waiting for your call."

"You won't believe who I saw down here a few minutes ago," said Rev. Baul excitedly.

"Not the journalist was it?" asked Musa, holding out the phone so the others could catch pieces of the other end of the conversation.

"In the flesh," he replied dramatically. "I followed him around for a while and sure enough I think he has gotten some tip about a possible case of bird flu, at least he was talking about a big secret."

"How could he have found that out?" asked Musa. "We told no one."

"The only thing I can think of is he made his way to the airport and did some snooping around," suggested Rev. Baul. "Or would he have overheard my telephone call to the medevac company? I felt ethically obligated to tell them the nature of our suspicions in order to make the evacuation appear as necessary as it was."

"I think he was already on the rooftop when we arrived for breakfast," Musa replied. Grandpa Baul and the kids shook their heads in agreement. "Either way what is he saying to the race organizers?"

"That's the strange part," explained Rev. Baul. "He hasn't breathed a word of it to anyone except me. He didn't come right out and say it but strongly hinted that he 'knew my secret,' was the way he phrased it."

"Secret? What is he talking about?" asked Musa.

"There is definitely more to this guy than meets the eye," confirmed Rev. Baul. "Oddly enough though, our bird is not the only one missing. I'd say there are a dozen irate owners marching around demanding answers right now. This guy could throw the place into a panic if he reveals his suspicions, and he knows it."

"Do you think he's selected a few random birds for testing?" asked Musa.

"He wouldn't have a clue how to go about it, I'm sure," said Rev. Baul. "He doesn't seem comfortable around the birds and any of the obvious terminology I used seemed foreign to him though he wouldn't admit it. I'm not at all convinced he is here to cover the race."

"No, it must be something else. Let me brainstorm with the crew here and call you back. Is there any concern about the sandstorm blowing in?"

"Yes they're watching the wind direction closely but saying it's not sandstorm season so either way it should blow through before lift off tomorrow morning. Any word from Kubri?" asked Rev. Baul.

"Not yet, but he'll probably call you first," Musa signed off and rallied the others to process any other possible angles the journalist might be using.

"I didn't want to mention Mrs. Baul's dilemma quite yet," admitted Musa. "Do you think I should have?"

"Definitely not," Grandpa Baul said emphatically.

"Hello! Kubri here," Rev. Baul heard a familiar voice coming through his satellite phone.

"Kubri!" exclaimed Rev. Baul. "It's so good to hear from you. You won't believe what's happening here."

"Really? I have big news too," said Kubri.

"Were you able to arrange a meeting with anyone on the Siwan counsel?"

"Better," said Kubri. "I'll fill you in soon. What have you found out?"

"I can't talk here," explained Rev. Baul. "Can we meet somewhere soon?"

"Yes, there is someone you need to meet," said Kubri looking over at his new friend Haj Sayed. "Can you get to the center square of town right across from the Shali ruins?"

"Sure, I'm only a five minute walk away. I'll be right there."

"Great," said Kubri. "I'm at an outside café. I'll call Musa and update him too."

Kubri hung up and ordered another coffee before dialing the monitoring control center. He gave Haj Sayed a few more details on Musa and the rest of the gang but had already filled him in fully on his friend Rev. Baul and his beloved wife, *Gameelah*.

"Musa, Kubri here," he said.

"Hello! We've been wondering how you are doing," Musa replied eagerly.

"I just spoke with Rev. Baul and he's heading my way," explained Kubri. "I've met a wonderfully knowledgeable man here who is willing to help our cause."

"Wow. That's sure great news," Musa breathed an audible sigh of relief as Grandpa and the kids tuned in. "We have enough fires to fight already."

"Where is Mrs. Baul right now?" asked Kubri.

"We got her exact GPS whereabouts from her phone but don't really understand what is going on," explained Musa. "It sounds like her camel caravan leader has deserted their whole group out in the middle of nowhere."

"What?" Kubri's voice sounded alarmed. "Rev. Baul doesn't know does he?"

"No, we didn't feel we should tell him yet," explained Musa.

"Good thinking," agreed Kubri. "I'll break the news to him tactfully. Who was in charge of the caravan?"

"The lodge manager arranged it but I don't know his name myself."

"Can you find out and get back to me?" asked Kubri. "I want to run it by my Siwan friend here."

"Sure, I'll call you right back," said Musa. "Did Rev. Baul tell you about the journalist and his threat to reveal a big secret?"

"What big secret? Do you think he's talking about the bird flu scare? How would he have known about that?" asked Kubri.

"We're guessing maybe he went to the airport or hired someone to eavesdrop on a telephone call?" Musa suggested. "We aren't sure that is all he knows or if that really is what he meant when he said he knew Rev. Baul's secret. It sounded like he was threatening him. That was also his tactic with Grandpa Baul in the hotel lobby earlier when he was snooping around after recognizing the Radcliffes."

"You're kidding?" said Kubri. "I'll get that story from him when he gets here soon."

"*Magnoon* Abdu?" Haj Sayed's face displayed a look of shock, then humor and finally settled for mild concern.

"Who is he?" asked Rev. Baul, now sipping coffee with Haj Sayed and Kubri.

"He is a mentally challenged man around here. Crazy Abdu he's called. Quite harmless really but he has been known to traumatize tourists before."

"What exactly do you mean by traumatize?" asked Rev. Baul whose voice began to quiver at the thought of his wife in the hands of this unknown man.

"He won't harm them physically, Rev. Baul," reassured Haj Sayed. "Several years back he was caught trying to rob tourists by taking them into the desert, deserting them for a few hours until they panicked, and then reappearing and demanding huge fees to return them back safely."

"That's horrible," exclaimed Rev. Baul. "We can't have that. Who knows what my wife may do?"

"Do you think he could be involved in the missing bishop affair?" asked Kubri.

"I really don't think so but it's too soon to say," mused Haj Sayed. "He doesn't seem bright enough to pull off a stunt like that. Like I said, he is harmless but mentally a little mixed up."

"I don't like the sound of it," reiterated Rev. Baul.

"Neither do I," admitted Haj Sayed. "What is he doing back out on the caravan trail? His camels had been confiscated and he was back under the protection of his family last I heard."

"Musa said the lodge manager was shocked to hear the tour group owner say he was giving *Magnoon* Abdu another chance," pointed out Kubri. He is a rehabilitated relative, or something along that line."

"Dreadful," exclaimed Haj Sayed. "Do not worry Rev. Baul. Your wife will be unharmed. The brewing storm may be of greater concern."

"Haj Sayed, with the swirling mysteries around my lovely wife these days I almost feel more concerned for *Magnoon* Abdu." The brief laughter temporarily diffused the tone of stress in their voices, yet all still sensed the deep concern in his manner.

"Do not fear," Haj Sayed's calming voice continued. "I must get in touch with my contacts to see how we should proceed with *Magnoon* Abdu and to ask if I can get permission to pay a visit to the tenting headquarters of the boys being initiated. No interruption is ever allowed except in extreme emergencies. The group has never been interrupted in my lifetime that I'm aware of. They protect this time as sacred, a training foundation for all of life. But instinct is telling me that contact with them will be important in solving the problems at hand."

"Thank you so much for your willingness to help us," Rev. Baul had warmed to his kindly spirit as Kubri joined in voicing his appreciation as well.

"Let us meet back here in two hours," declared Haj Sayed. "I should be able to have more answers in place by then."

Kubri and Rev. Baul shook hands again with their new friend and sat back down to make their own plans.

"We should go back to the lodge and talk to the others," said Rev. Baul.

"You're right," agreed Kubri. "These next few hours will be critical."

-19-

Espionage at large

"Yes, Bishop Kareem!" exclaimed Rev. Baul. "What a pleasant surprise. I planned to update you on our happenings here as soon as I had gathered more facts."

"We have a very large problem Rev. Baul," warned the bishop, before launching into his reason for calling.

"What is it Bishop Kareem?"

"I have been notified by the EU that Madame Napoleon has been checked into the hospital here in Cairo and her husband is in route to join her," he began. "A physician friend of mine at the hospital has discretely informed me of their initial suspicions concerning this bird flu diagnosis, but nothing has been leaked to the press because of the countrywide repercussions if it is."

"I'm grateful for that," noted Rev. Baul.

"The problem lies in an unsealed letter the physician was handed when checking Madame Napoleon into the hospital. You understand that for legal reasons they are required to search the patient's purse to confirm identification upon arrival?"

"Yes, that would make sense," Rev. Baul added, still in confusion as to the very large problem.

"Knowing my high profile position with the international media on the missing bishop case, this doctor kindly had the letter delivered to my office before turning it over to EU headquarters and consequently the eager international media. He felt it too urgent to wait until Monsieur Napoleon was able to return to Cairo."

"What is in the letter?" asked Rev. Baul

"This is the dilemma," explained the bishop. "Let me read it to you."

Press Release:

- Terrorist Cell Uncovered
- Weapons of Mass Destruction
- Kidnapped Bishop's Whereabouts Discovered

"Oh no," groaned Rev. Baul. "Who has read it besides you, Bishop Kareem?"

"Only the physician, a trusted man," he explained. "But I need to find out two things from you there. Is there any truth in her written accusations and is it possible she has already faxed this to a news organization?"

Rev. Baul was silent for a moment. "Bishop Kareem, I know for certain her first two accusations are erroneous, but I have been told since arriving here in Siwa that she and Madame Napoleon were trying to track down the missing bishop and were convinced he was somewhere in or near Siwa."

"What does your friend Kubri think?" asked the bishop.

"He thinks it's very probable Edwin is in the area and still alive," Rev. Baul replied. "We have a trusted Siwan helping us now. There is only one journalist still around so I'd say that we would already have heard about it in the media if that press release draft had been sent somewhere."

"Good point."

The bishop seemed greatly relieved at that reasoning. He went on to explain he'd had a long conversation with the Archbishop of Canterbury that morning about the status of the search for Edwin. "His mother in London is frantic but has been comforted by a representative sent by MI6 who is a kidnapping expert. His team's analysis is that none of the signs of his disappearance follow classic patterns. There has been no attempt to seek out a ransom or get media attention."

"I see their reasoning," said Rev. Baul. "Bishop Kareem, I feel terrible about the whole fiasco. I am determined to find my friend and I know we have the best chance possible with the contact we've made here."

"Thank you Rev. Baul. I trust your judgment. I will not pass on this letter," assured the bishop. "If you were already aware of the situation and have kept silent then I will do likewise for now."

"Thank you Bishop Kareem. I will get back to you as soon as I know more."

"Call me day or night. I am here for you."

Rev. Baul immediately called his father with details of the bishop's call as well as Haj Sayed's description of *Magnoon* Abdu. Grandpa Baul could sense the strain in his son's voice, knowing more than just his reputation was on the line. He loved his wife dearly and knew her intentions were admirable, but events had certainly escalated out of control. In one sense it was merciful that Sir Peter and Lady Sarah had removed Madame Napoleon from the center of action. Hopefully her diagnosis would prove benign in the end. They must stay focused at present and work toward finding Mrs. Baul.

"I might be mistaken but that sure looks like a disorganized kit of racing pigeons flying overhead." Mrs. Baul's observation boomed through the tech center's voice monitoring system. She had obviously retraced her steps to rejoin the others.

"Lady, you must be high on something really exotic." The voice of the disgruntled Australian tourist could be heard again.

"Be kind, darling," his female companion reprimanded. "I know you are frightened but so are we all."

"I'm not frightened," he lashed back. "I'm just angry at this dusty desert dweller for dangling us out to dry."

"I have a GPS tracker on my satellite phone," announced Mrs. Baul.

"Well, why didn't you say so sooner, lady? I'm parched and this blowing sand is killing my eyes. Let's get ourselves out of here," growled the man.

"I would have mentioned it earlier but I haven't had a chance to read the thick manual I left back at the lodge. I have no idea how to do anything with it except place phone calls," she admitted.

"Let me see that thing," demanded the tourist. "For starters, it looks like your battery is almost gone. That's real swift planning."

"Oh dear," Mrs. Baul moaned. "I better place a call to my sick friend. I only have one phone number saved in the memory file and it's hers."

"Grandpa, should we call her?" Miriam panicked. "I'm starting to feel sorry for her."

"Don't worry Miriam. We won't loose her location even if her battery goes out because she isn't going anywhere for the moment," reassured Grandpa. "Sir Peter and Lady Sarah are standing by and we can get there quickly by jeep."

"Why don't we then, Grandpa?" asked Joe.

"It may come to that soon but it would jeopardize further reconnaissance. We're so close to a break through. There's a real possibility this caravan leader may lead us to the missing bishop and we cannot put that possibility at risk," he explained.

"But Grandpa, it sounds like she's going to try to call Madame Napoleon," worried Miriam.

"I have her phone right here, remember?" said Musa, very relieved Lady Sarah had taken that precaution before leaving for the airport.

"Joe, it may be time to put those acting classes into practice," suggested Grandpa.

"Cool, you really mean it?"

"Why not? All you have to do is mimic a high voice with a British accent," explained Grandpa Baul. "The fact that your mother left her friend weak and feverish will cover over any lack of recognition."

Miriam laughed at her brother's first attempt. They all clapped whenever he achieved anything close to perfection.

By the time Madame Napoleon's phone rang, complete silence had overtaken the group.

"Hello?" squeaked Joe in a disoriented voice.

"My friend is that you? I hope you are feeling much better," Mrs. Baul began. "I am so sorry to have deserted you this morning but it was imperative that we make headway today. I hope you understand."

"Of course, darling," Joe continued. Respectfully no one looked at Joe while he was talking to ensure he didn't break into laughter. "I am still sick though."

"Oh, I'm so sorry to hear that. I hope to be back soon to help you but I have gotten myself into a quandary. Our plan to get embedded with a camel caravan line seems to have backfired."

Miriam had to completely turn her back to her brother and tried not to let her shaking shoulders distract his concentration.

"What seems to be . . . hello? Hello? Are you there?" Joe turned toward the others. "Her phone's dead."

"Mister Baul?" came a voice at their lodge room's door followed by another unfamiliar knock.

"Yes, coming," called Grandpa Baul in what seemed like a déjà vu.

"The front desk manager wants to see you, Mister Baul."

"Thank you," Grandpa Baul replied. "I will be there soon."

He closed the door again and the group discussed possible scenarios. In the end they all agreed he should just go talk to the manager. They didn't think it likely that he would know about the disappearance of *Magnoon* Abdu yet.

"Hello my friend," Grandpa Baul greeted the manager cheerily in the currently full lobby of the lodge. "I hear you have a message for me."

"Yes, I do," he said. "Let me help check in these people and I will join you on the veranda for a cup of tea, my compliments."

"Thank you," said Grandpa Baul. "I'll be happy to have some refreshment."

Shortly the manager left the care of the arriving guests in the hands of his assistants and joined Grandpa Baul outside. He explained that every single guest showing up that afternoon was registered as a reporter or journalist of some sort. This was not tourist season in spite of the weekend's bird race. Although he knew the pigeon race was newsworthy within Egypt proper, he had his suspicions that the people with passports he was registering had nothing to do with birds.

Grandpa Baul felt the timing was right to enlighten the manager on the *Magnoon* Abdu developments.

"I am shocked, Mr. Baul," said the manager very apologetically. "Such an arrangement was against my authority. That caravan tour agency has an excellent reputation. I do not understand why they would have such a person in their employ."

"You aren't at fault," assured Grandpa. "What is your opinion on the impending sandstorm? Can we venture out into the desert right now?"

"I strongly advise against going far into the sand sea at this point in the day," he said. "Because Mrs. Baul and the other tourists are on the caravan tour I will contact the tourist police office immediately to get jeeps deployed for a search and rescue effort. I assure you this will be sorted out before sundown."

"Thank you sir."

"I beg of you to keep this information confidential or the hovering journalists will wreak havoc on our reputations," pleaded the manager.

"You have my word," confirmed Grandpa. The last thing any of them needed were more prying questions.

When Grandpa Baul arrived back at headquarters he found Kubri had returned and was debriefing the others. In agreement with their continued attempt to keep Rev. Baul from full knowledge of their surveillance capability Kubri had diplomatically arranged for a debriefing with the others on the rooftop, provided they had the place to themselves. That would leave them a few minutes to freshen up and regroup before the scheduled rendezvous with Haj Sayed in an hour.

"Rev. Baul, I thought I might find you here," exclaimed the all too familiar stalking journalist.

"Hello again, sir. How did you know I was here?" queried Rev. Baul, concerned that strangers were scrutinizing his movements. He paused to rub his eyes, as the blowing winds seemed to be picking up, and motioned toward the protection of the rooftop awning creatively designed with palm tree beams and draped with dried woven branches.

"A front desk clerk overheard you talking," the journalist explained, joining him at a sheltered corner table.

"What can I do for you?" asked Rev. Baul in a reserved yet polite tone of voice.

"Some very valuable information has come into my hands and you may want to comment on it before I report back to my agency." explained the man.

"What could that have to do with me?" asked Rev. Baul nervously.

"Not you, Reverend, but your wife."

"My wife? You leave my lovely wife out of your snooping," insisted Rev. Baul, his cheeks beginning to flush with color. "I don't believe you are a journalist here to cover the pigeon race. What are you really doing here?"

"First of all I am not at liberty to say anything more than that I have been commissioned by, what your laymen's terms might call, a 'nuke watchdog' branch of the European Union," he elaborated. "They received potentially compromising information that needed to be confirmed. All leads are pointing in the direction of your wife, Rev. Baul."

"This is absurd," he countered. "My wife is as innocent and pure hearted as they come. I am the first to admit she does have an artistic imagination, but quite harmless I assure you."

At this point in the conversation the man turned to see the rest of Rev. Baul's entourage arrive as if on cue. Obviously he did not want to continue the conversation in the company of the others so Rev. Baul was granted a reprieve for the moment. The man stood, nodded his head respectfully in the direction of the newcomers, and retreated back down the stairs.

"What was that about, son?" asked Grandpa Baul curiously.

"Hopefully nothing," said Rev. Baul. "If I'm not mistaken I think he may have been hinting at accusing my wife of espionage. Imagine!"

-20-

Tracking trails of sand

"May I have your attention everyone?" Mrs. Baul's voice was coming through loud and clear. Musa had agreed to stay with the listening machinery in case anything new developed while the others were gone. Thankfully Mrs. Baul had not removed her bracelet but volume reception was at the mercy of her many arm movements.

"Gather around please everyone," she requested again.

The other members of the expedition, only half a dozen in all, were trying to determine what their next move should be. Some were already complaining of thirst and sand grit in their eyes and teeth, so the remaining bottles brought along for the journey were carefully rationed out. The increasing winds were clearly bothering them all. Mrs. Baul began to think about Moses and his 40 years of wandering in the Sinai. How did he manage such a feat?

"I believe we need to come to a decision as to what we should do next," she began. "Do we want to stay put and wait for our leader to hopefully return or should we set out after him?"

"Follow him," cried one woman.

"He's not coming back," yelled another.

"We're doomed to die," shouted a woman about Mrs. Baul's age.

"We will not be dying," Mrs. Baul assured them with firm resolution. "I could still make out his trail from the top of the dune, but with the blowing sand it will not be long before those tracks disappear. If we're going to move it must be now."

"What about trying to get back where we came from?" this calm suggestion came from what Musa assumed was the Australian woman. "I think if we head northeast we should hit the edge of the oasis again. We really didn't travel that far. Maybe two or three hours at most."

"Hear! Hear!" cried her companion. "I don't want to be buried in a sand blizzard."

"I say we put it to a vote," Mrs. Baul continued.

From the bits and pieces that were coming across the sound frequency waves Musa assumed the vote had been unanimous to turn back. He was shocked to hear Mrs. Baul's announcement.

"It may be a wise decision to turn back, although if the sandstorm continues to build what is left of the sun will be impossible to follow. It may be wiser to remain here and dig in until nightfall and then follow the stars," Mrs. Baul suggested. "I myself have more at stake here than you all realize and I must leave you and follow our deserter as I believe he will lead me to my reason for joining this caravan in the first place."

"Oh no!" sputtered Musa out loud. "Now what do we do?"

"No, ma'am, that is not a sound decision," the Australian woman called out.

"I knew you were a spy," shouted her companion.

"I cannot say more, but I wish you all the best of luck."

Musa guessed Mrs. Baul must have mounted her camel at that point from the sounds he was receiving.

"Sir Peter? Musa calling."

"Musa, we've been waiting for your call!" he announced eagerly.

"I can't talk long because I need to update the others, but Mrs. Baul is on the move again," he explained. "She is still at the spot where we received her last GPS signal before her phone died."

"Her phone died out?" groaned Sir Peter.

"The nightmare escalates. Mrs. Baul has abandoned the rest of her convoy and is heading south I'm guessing."

"Do you have a topographical map or bigger picture of the area?" asked Sir Peter.

"Yes, from the satellite imaging I have I'm guessing that *Magnoon* Abdu guy knew exactly what he was doing and fled the scene heading toward the cold spring further southeast," Musa explained. "I don't know why he was talking about the hot springs to the others because from what we've heard, their bubbling levels of sulfur are only wooing mosquitoes."

"Could just have been a ruse to throw them off track," Sir Peter suggested.

"That's possible but it's not as if these tourists know the lay of the land. At any rate the hot springs look like they are still further southwest but not any farther away than the cold spring. There are probably a few big dunes blocking clear views of either of the springs but their current position doesn't look very far off at all. I think the guy purposely dumped them between the two so he had options of his own."

"How far away do you think the springs are by camel?"

"Less than a mile and even taking the weather into consideration I'd say easily under an hour for a camel to cover. Mrs. Baul thinks she's hot on his trail but that trail will be long blown over by the time she remounts that dune with her camel. He could easily have left prints in one direction and knowing the wind, changed direction immediately to lose any upset followers."

"So should we head straight for the cold spring and apprehend the guy?"

"No, let me give you her last coordinates and you can head that way first. The lodge manager is asking the police to coordinate a search and rescue effort but according to Kubri the tourist police are legally bound to steer clear of the place where the tribal leaders have set up camp for the initiation rites or things could get very dicey."

"Don't tell me their camp is at the cold spring?" Sir Peter's pessimism was getting the best of him.

"Naturally, Sir Peter," Musa replied echoing his cynicism.

"Okay. As far as Lady Sarah and I are concerned we've never heard of such anthropological eccentricities."

"It's not so easy as that Sir Peter," Musa warned. "We've been told that not only is the presence of foreigners forbidden but if any woman were ever to interrupt their ritual withdrawal there would be bloodshed to pay."

"Humph." Sir Peter replied. "Sarah is well disguised, I assure you. I would request the presence of Miriam's linguistic talents but under the threatening circumstances I will not risk putting her in harm's way. We've already made some progress and we're heavily armed with satellite phones, medical supplies, and high-tech prayer beads."

"You're going to need to hurry, Sir Peter. If Mrs. Baul trots into that camp on her camel I don't know what we'll be able to do about it. Godspeed." Musa hung up and dialed Grandpa Baul's number.

Musa was able to reach Grandpa Baul by phone. He did not want to leave his monitoring job, so he called with as many details as he could remember. He now needed to pay attention to the Radcliffe's progress as well. Thankfully the latest weather report promised a change in wind direction. That would certainly help with visibility and tracking, let alone provide less discomfort to the wilderness wanderers. Within minutes Musa could hear Sir Peter trying out his prayer beads.

"Testing one, two, three. Testing," a chuckling Lady Sarah could distinctly be heard in the background.

Musa welcomed the comic relief and assured his companions he was with them in spirit. Rev. Baul and Kubri were no doubt back in route to Siwa's town center to find out how Haj Sayed was progressing. Grandpa Baul, Miriam and Joe returned to debrief with Musa in person, hoping their chance for a more active role in the dangerous desert adventure had finally arrived.

"Hello Haj Sayed," called Kubri with Rev. Baul mirroring his welcome.

"So good to see you again, my friends," Haj Sayed greeted them warmly. "Much has blown over the dunes, so to speak, since I saw you last."

"We're very eager to hear," Rev. Baul replied.

"First of all, the local police have been brought in to search for your missing caravan, which I think you already knew from your lodge manager's request," he explained. "I have made contact with the acting tribal chiefs in the village here and been given permission to travel alone to their camp to make inquiries. I pushed hard to be able to take you with me but my request was denied emphatically. I am sorry."

"I can respect that arrangement," said Rev. Baul kindly. "We are just so grateful for your trust and assistance in the matter."

"Were you able to ask any questions about the search for the missing bishop?" asked Kubri.

"Yes, in fact I did probe for information and I can assure you that no united tribal Siwan effort whatsoever has been made, in spite of the initial pressure from international journalists and perhaps some exploration by random tourist police," explained Haj Sayed. "Because of the timing and the tribal leaders being inaccessible, even their camp headquarters is unaware of a missing person at large."

"Wow. And here we thought the searched area had been exhausted so the press moved on," said Rev. Baul.

"Well then, there is still hope on that front," exclaimed Kubri. "If only haphazard searches have been mounted so far then there is every reason to believe we may still find him."

"I think because I won't be able to accompany you, Haj Sayed, it is past time I check on my pigeon racers," Rev. Baul explained. "If there is any chance my missing pigeon

Mrs. Baul Investigates

may return I would like to be there to welcome him home safely to his cage."

"Goodbye then for now friend," said Haj Sayed.

"I will be in touch by phone soon," Kubri assured him.

Haj Sayed sensed Kubri's desire for him to stay put until Rev. Baul had gone on his way.

"I need to update you on the most recent movements of Mrs. Baul, my *Gameelah*, just in case any awkward circumstances arise," began Kubri in a self-conscious whisper.

They discussed the situation thoroughly. Because Haj Sayed's diplomatic trip to the desert was already risky Kubri did not feel it was appropriate to request his compliance with high tech surveillance; neither did he want to use deceit to obtain it. Musa already had satellite coordinates for a cold spring they all assumed was the epicenter of this whole affair. It was by far the closest spring to civilization yet far enough out for complete desert silence. Before leaving, Haj Sayed gave Kubri a time and place for their next rendezvous and left him with a blessing for peace and success.

"Well, look there," Mrs. Baul was apparently now talking to her humped means of transport. "If that isn't the pigeons again. They seem to be sweeping the area quite deliberately. Perhaps they have found water and we should follow them."

Fortunately for Musa and the other listening ears, Mrs. Baul was lonely without the rest of the group and was voicing her every move. After reaching the top of the dune she had climbed on foot, it appeared that the prints she'd been intent on following had faded into what could have been mistaken as a long crease folded over by the wind. Mrs. Baul sounded momentarily disoriented. But as predicted, the winds had changed direction and calmed significantly and this gave her renewed confidence. She set out on the course she vaguely remembered seeing, yet the next sandy hilltop vista refused to reveal the secret of the caravan leader's mysterious escape route.

"I wonder if one of those pigeons belongs to my husband?" she murmured. "Perhaps he is sending me a message by pigeon post!"

"Grandpa, I think she's become delusional," Miriam complained.

"Heatstroke or windblown to the max?" suggested Joe.

"Patience kids, her verbal trail is our only hope," confirmed Grandpa. "It's such a shame we've completely lost her location."

"Musa, can't we hire a helicopter or something and go searching?" asked Joe.

"That's one of the stipulations of the tribal council, Joe," explained Musa. "No helicopters are even allowed to land at the little airport here in Siwa and no air traffic at all can fly through the airspace of these sacred sand seas south of the oasis."

"Good logical thinking though," Grandpa added encouragingly.

Minutes passed by before Mrs. Baul's camel successfully mounted the next wave of sand.

"Well, I don't believe my eyes," she called out with great delight. "Would you look at those trees way off in the distance? There must be water there unless I'm seeing a mirage. And there are the birds again!"

"What is she seeing Musa?" asked Grandpa Baul.

"I'm not sure. Could be that both those springs in the region have trees springing up but I'd be more inclined to picture large brush along the edges. I don't think these are very large reservoirs of water."

"Musa, what about trying out the microscopic tracker on the pigeon's beak?" suggested Miriam. "Do you have that gear with you?"

"I brought all my portable equipment along. You know I've never really tested it out in field conditions though."

"Great idea Miriam," said Grandpa. "Why don't you just give it a try, Musa? What do we have to lose?"

"Well, for one thing I think my GPS pigeon beak invention isn't perfected enough to take a proper reading while they're in flight." said Musa. "But if they've found water then that should be just what we need."

"Mister Baul," came another knock on the door.

"Coming," Grandpa Baul called as he opened the door and stepped into the hallway.

"There is news for you at the front desk," reported the man.

"I will come back with you. Thank you for coming to get me."

"Big news Mr. Baul," the ecolodge manager greeted him eagerly. "The police have apprehended *Magnoon* Abdu."

"So quickly?" queried Grandpa Baul. "What about the others he deserted?"

"Before he is handed over to the acting Siwan council for questioning he is being forced to help the local police track down his lost caravan. The police have jeeps and the travelers will not have wandered far. I'm sure they will be found very soon," the manager assured him.

"Thank you so much for your swift efforts, sir." Grandpa Baul did not think it wise to enlighten him further on the now missing Mrs. Baul. Clearly the tourist police knew their business but the wavering lines of their jurisdiction posed insurmountable problems at present.

"Please let me know what more I can do."

"Would you mind letting the jeep driver I hired for the day know that I am finally ready to set out for an afternoon drive?" requested Grandpa Baul.

"Certainly, I will let you know when he arrives. The sandstorm has thankfully blown over."

As Grandpa Baul headed in the direction of his room he caught the eye of the familiar journalist now chatting in the lobby with others in his similar employ. Thankfully he made a direct line for the manager rather than for himself. That could keep them all distracted and off their backs for a while.

N 29°07'19.83"
E 25°26'01.91"

Musa read the numbers off to the others. Grandpa Baul scooped up his equipment bag, signaled his grandchildren and darted out the door; whether the coordinates were completely accurate or not it was as good a place to start as any.

-21-

Mrs. Baul digs deeper

"Look at that scene," Mrs. Baul announced to her camel. "How strange. It looks like there's concrete around the edge of that small pool of water. Hardly what I imagined as an exotic desert spring."

"Mrs. Baul has stumbled onto something," Musa said as Kubri's ears tuned in as well to the sound of her pronouncement.

After seeing Haj Sayed off on his trek to the cold spring encampment and knowing Rev. Baul would be well occupied with pigeon race affairs, Kubri returned to help Musa coordinate what had now evolved into a complicated surveillance endeavor.

"I wonder where she is?" asked Kubri.

"I doubt it's the cold spring or she would have seen tents and been apprehended long before she spotted water, I would guess," suggested Musa.

"Oh dear, look at that, a dead pigeon," Mrs. Baul moaned. "This is just too much. I can't take anymore. My nerves are shot from the strain of this espionage business."

"Oh, oh," said Musa.

"Bird flu?" asked Kubri.

"Probably not, but it's mandatory now to collect any dead fowl for examination just in case," he explained. "If those are really pigeons that had been entered in the race and escaped I doubt this bird is the only carrier."

"Would you look at that? The other birds are leaving him and flying away. I wonder if there is something they didn't like about the water?" Mrs. Baul's camel seemed to be listening intently and produced a noise that sounded like yelling and spitting rolled into one. "Let's get a bit closer and see what you think of the water. You must be ready for a drink by now."

"I have to take my hat off to my *Gameelah*, it's not every amateur rider who can hold her own with such a creature," said Kubri.

"I doubt her camel is anywhere near ready for a drink though if it was well watered recently," added Musa.

"I agree with you. It seems to have a bit of an odd smell," commented Mrs. Baul. "I wonder why there's steam rising out of the water?"

"Hot springs!" declared Kubri.

"Yes, and if the bird reading was accurate we've got those coordinates as confirmation," exclaimed Musa. "Let's call our crew and update them."

"Now which direction did those birds fly off?" Mrs. Baul was refocusing her efforts. "Let's get to the top of this next ridge and take a look around."

"Thank you Musa," said Grandpa Baul. "That's helpful information. We'll be on it as soon as we can get this overheated jeep back in action. The minute we hit the deep dunes just outside of town the thing started steaming."

"You're kidding?" replied Musa.

"This vehicle is a good thirty years old," explained Grandpa. "The knob on the gearshift is long gone and the interior looks like bare bones. It's amazing it runs at all, but our driver assures us it's no problem. Overheats all the time."

"Does he have extra water along?" asked Musa.

"Yes, quite a few full bottles, but he's talking about needing to refill them at a spring out here," added Grandpa Baul.

"Okay, stay on course. We'll check back in soon," said Musa. "Over and out."

"Grandpa, can I try out the sand board while we're waiting?" asked Joe.

"Of course! It may take some practice to get the hang of it," said Grandpa.

Joe climbed to the top of the nearest dune and faced his board toward the others. His first run immediately grounded him face first in sand. He got up spitting and sputtering as Grandpa and Miriam watched in amusement. Miriam was half way up the dune by then and threw him a pair of goggles before joining him on another board. She managed to sail past him before the shock of a dive greeted her.

"This is great!" she called back toward Grandpa, still spitting sand but happy to stop and model a wide sandy grin for Grandpa's camera.

"Grandpa, you need to try this out," called Joe. "At least try some sledding."

"I will before the day's out," he called back.

Soon their driver slammed down the hood of the jeep and motioned for them to climb in the back. Grandpa stuck to riding in the front for the view, he said. His grandchildren were guessing it was so he could brace himself for the steep roller coaster rides they were taking at neck breaking speeds. The back of their jeep looked like a converted flatbed with low-rise benches and a canopy of canvas to shield them from sun. There wasn't much to hold onto on the downhill rides, but the thrill of the adventure was what they were after.

"Hey look there, Grandpa," yelled Joe through the open cab window of the car. "That looks like a camel caravan off in the distance."

"Yeah," shouted Miriam over the noise of the windy ride.

"Good eyes, kids," confirmed Grandpa as he pointed the driver in the caravan's direction. "I won't be surprised if they belong to *Magnoon* Abdu."

"*Magnoon* Abdu?" asked the wide-eyed driver. Miriam explained briefly what had happened to the tour group earlier in the day. Clearly some sort of legend surrounded the man but the driver would not comment further.

"Musa, can you take another reading of the pigeon's location?" asked Kubri.

"Good idea. Let's give it a try."

"No, nothing coming through," said Musa after several tries. "They must be in flight. I wish I'd spent more time perfecting this device."

"No problem. Do you have coordinates for the cold spring?" asked Kubri.

"I have some satellite images but it looks like there are half a dozen spots of water in the area," explained Musa. "My best guess for the encampment would be the closest one to Siwa."

"Haj Sayed certainly thought they wouldn't have gone far," said Kubri.

"Wow. What a beautiful expanse of creation," declared Mrs. Baul. She was certainly back in good spirits for all she had gone through in the course of the day. "I can see why this is called a sand sea. These waves go on forever."

"She must be at the top of a ridge," said Kubri, stating the obvious.

"Now what could that be way over there? Very curious," Mrs. Baul mused.

"What is she seeing?" asked Musa.

"Speak to us, my *Gameelah*," Kubri pleaded into the one-way receptor.

"I think we need to head in that direction," Mrs. Baul continued. "I don't see the birds anymore but whatever that is off in the distance is very odd indeed."

"She must still be pretty far off if she can't identify it," said Musa.

"I suppose. I'm not good at patient surveillance. Much rather be out in the field," Kubri added.

"I hear you. Wish I had my mobile felucca about now," said Musa. "If I lived out here I'd have to gear up a jeep or a moving tent or something."

"How about inventing camel collars with GPS built in?" Kubri laughed himself out of his irritable mood.

"I think we should let our driver do the talking," suggested Miriam as they drew nearer to the camels riding toward them. "On second thought, they all look like westerners."

"Hello there," called Grandpa once they had narrowed the gap.

All the travelers were waving wildly as if the jeep that was heading straight for them was an airplane zooming over a deserted island with little chance of recognition. The relief on their faces was evident. Mrs. Baul was not among them, as expected, but they immediately related her odd behavior and concern that she would never be found. One woman mentioned her conversation about a kidnapped bishop and another man stated she was an undercover spy. Miriam and Joe barely maintained their serious search and rescue composure when Grandpa Baul treated them to a reassuring wink.

"Let's get you down from there and give you some water," offered Grandpa Baul. "We've got some emergency bottles stocked in the back of our jeep."

"Thank you," came a chorus of weary voices as they started the process of dismounting.

"The police are out searching for you all," explained Grandpa. "I'll call in your location to my friend and he'll get them pointed in your direction right way."

Grandpa Baul's demeanor was obviously comforting to the group. They wandered around in the sand bowlegged while they stretched their sore muscles and then eagerly drank down the offered water. A few of the tourists seemed disgruntled and exhausted but nothing that re-hydration and a night's rest wouldn't cure. Most were stepping up to the occasion and already collaborating with details. The news of *Magnoon* Abdu's identity and subsequent capture was a jaw-dropping scenario they could hardly believe.

"I knew there was something fishy about that guy from the beginning," muttered a man with an Australian accent. The Baul children locked eyes in recognition of the voice that had ridiculed their dear mother.

"I've confirmed your search and rescue crew are on the way," confirmed Grandpa Baul after finishing a phone conversation. "They'll be taking you back to Siwa by vehicle and are bringing out a man who will rope and guide the camels back to town."

Although Grandpa Baul did not want to waste anymore time waiting around for the rescue team to arrive it did not seem appropriate to desert these vulnerable people twice in one day and to leave the camels unattended. Musa had given them the latest disturbing update on the movements of Mrs. Baul, but they would deal with that shortly. The Radcliffes' progress was confirmed. Unfortunately there was no word from Haj Sayed, but of course that would have to wait until the scheduled rendezvous.

With the discovery of the missing caravan, *Magnoon* Abdu was immediately released into the care of his family with the guarantee that he would appear before the Siwan council for questioning. His punishment would most likely be a mild form of house arrest, ensuring the tourist industry would not be jeopardized further, but kindly taking into account his essentially harmless behavior toward others.

-22-

The silencing of Mrs. Baul

Dull crimson clouds edged the horizon as Mrs. Baul's camel devotedly carried her forward. Time was beginning to whirl dizzily in her mind, making her unsure whether the colorful sky was ushering in dusk or dawn.

"Boy am I going to need to stretch my legs soon," Mrs. Baul's voice rejoined the listeners. "Now I'm starting to see red mirages. I wonder if I'll ever make it out of here alive."

"Red mirages?" asked Musa. "What could that be?"

Musa strained forward to try to decipher the garbled sounds.

"If I'm not mistaken that red thing looks like a half buried jeep," exclaimed Mrs. Baul. "Oh no! A jeep! My dream!" She caught her breath, put her hand to her heart and tried desperately to remain calm. Shifting herself into a more comfortable riding position she braced herself to move forward, determinedly crushing nightmare images of being drowned in an avalanche of sand.

"A jeep?" asked Kubri. "What dream?"

Mrs. Baul Investigates

"Who knows," said Musa. "Better a jeep than a tent."

"And look there on the other side of it I think I can make out the top of an old faded tent," Mrs. Baul continued.

"Ugh," said Musa.

"She's closing in," declared Kubri. "Maybe I need to get out there in case things get messy."

"No, the Radcliffes are in place and Haj Sayed is the best buffer we have," said Musa.

"True, but they might not be as close as she is right now," worried Kubri.

"Grandpa Baul is in range too."

"Okay, this is maddening," muttered Kubri. "I think we'll all deserve medals when this is over. How can my *Gameelah*, dear Madame Baul, put me through so much anxiety?"

"Welcome to life with the Bauls," Musa smiled warmly.

"Yes I'm sure of it now. That is definitely a jeep, and not an old rusted out one either," Mrs. Baul confirmed. "Oh dear. I do hope the Right Reverend isn't buried inside. Do we dare get a closer look? I have a dreadful feeling about this."

Minutes passed by as Musa and Kubri sat on the edge of their chairs full of tension. As her camel carried her closer to the scene of the jeep's demise, Mrs. Baul noticed two tied up camels resting in front of the abandoned half buried tent.

"Could it be our caravan deserter?" she asked her camel. "But he only rode off with his own camel. Maybe he was secretly meeting someone here." She slipped her shaking hand into her side pack and secured her small spray can of mace.

"*Salaam wa'alaykum*," came a deep man's voice while she watched in surprise as another emerged from the tent.

"*Wa'alaykum salaam*," she answered politely, desperately trying to appear calm.

"Who are you?" Mrs. Baul called out in English. "You are not my caravan leader. Have you seen a kidnapped bishop?"

The two men turned toward each other and launched into a long dialogue in Arabic, or perhaps Siwi.

"Where is my Miriam when I need her?" she muttered.

The men seemed dreadfully dangerous. Their faces were almost completely covered in their desert apparel. They could easily be the ones who had kidnapped the bishop. Mrs. Baul hesitated and almost turned to move on but the sight of drinking water bottles being waved in her direction were overwhelming to her dry throat. What did she have to lose? Worst case scenario she would be joining her friend the bishop, dead or alive. She held onto her mace tightly and commanded her camel to kneel. One of the men seemed to sense her reluctance so approached her with open hands, nodding and bowing his welcome. The other sinister-looking figure disappeared back into the tent. A dark premonition unexpectedly suffocated her voice.

"We've got her and she looks armed," a voice reported.

"Take her down then," commanded the listener.

"Musa?" Rev. Baul's voice was full of excitement.

"Good to hear from you," he answered, wondering at the timing of his call. He couldn't possibly know anything about Mrs. Baul's ominous situation. Not sure how to give a full explanation of the latest developments, he stalled, "Kubri and I are here at the lodge together. What's your news?"

"You'll never believe it but our prized pigeon has returned!"

"Really?" asked Musa. "That's amazing! Great news."

"He seems completely uninjured," Rev. Baul continued. "He was certainly thirsty but very happy to be reunited with his mate. They've just finished nesting and weaning babies back home, you know."

"Have any of the other pigeons returned?" asked Musa. It seemed absurd they were discussing pigeons when Mrs. Baul's life was hanging in the balance.

"Yes, most of them I think. And they seemed to have traveled together," explained Rev. Baul. "There is only one person here that seems annoyed that they've returned."

"That's your man then, Rev. Baul," Musa answered, trying intently to focus on what Rev. Baul was saying. "I'd report his suspicious behavior in a big hurry to the Race Secretary. What do his birds look like?"

"Not great, that's for sure," Rev. Baul noted. "I agree it's worth reporting."

Musa put his hand over the phone so Rev. Baul couldn't hear his question to Kubri.

"Should I tell him about his wife?" he asked.

"I don't think the timing is right," said Kubri. "There is nothing we can do about it right now anyway."

"What about the rescue of *Magnoon* Abdu's crew?" asked Musa.

"Not until Mrs. Baul is safe," suggested Kubri. "No need to worry him further."

Musa nodded agreement.

"Thanks for the good news, friend," concluded Musa. "I think you should stay and watch over developments there. Kubri says hello too."

"Okay, thank you both. If I'm not mistaken I see the head of our journalist friend making his way toward me," said Rev. Baul.

"Just keep him focused on pigeons for now," suggested Musa.

"Will do. Talk to you soon."

The two camel riders carefully heaved Mrs. Baul's body onto an old carpet and dragged her into their tent. They tied her camel up with the others and dialed a satellite phone.

"Grandpa Baul. Peter here. We've got Mrs. Baul secured. Call Musa for our exact location."

"We're on our way," Grandpa Baul replied as he swung into action. The police rescue team had arrived just minutes before so they were free to move on.

"What is it Grandpa?" asked Joe eagerly.

"Your mother is out of harm's way."

"Well, give us the details, Grandpa," begged Miriam.

"Let me call Musa and get their coordinates first."

N 29°07'36.15"
E 25°26'48.11"

"Grandpa Baul, unless those satellite readings are mistaken they are practically right on top of the cold spring we've been looking for," explained Musa.

"Really?" he replied. "Sir Peter didn't mention she'd gotten that close."

"Maybe one more ridge over at most. According to Haj Sayed an obvious encampment of tents would be dotting the landscape."

"You can't be far at all from the hot springs either," explained Musa. "On your way back with the Radcliffes can you swing by there and check out a dead pigeon Mrs. Baul mentioned? I feel responsible to act on the information we've been given, what with the Madame Napoleon scare hanging in the balance."

"What's happening with Haj Sayed?" asked Grandpa.

"We have to wait patiently for his rendezvous with Kubri and Rev. Baul," explained Musa.

The Baul trio covered the distance quickly in their aged but tech-equipped jeep. The sun would be setting soon so time was short. Just as they were closing in on the Radcliffes' location, their driver pointed out a vast scene. Desert tents were spread all around a beautiful fresh water spring. Tall brush lined its edges and small campfires were being lit all about. The driver used the Arabic word *haraam* to confirm their presence was forbidden.

As soon as Sir Peter and Lady Sarah heard the approach of the jeep, they emerged from their cover to welcome their friends.

"She looks dead," stated Joe with great drama.

"Sleeping beauty is more like it," Lady Sarah pronounced.

"We were hoping to be able to use less dramatic means, like our tea spout tranquilizer, but your mom had some dangerous tricks up her sleeve," Sir Peter addressed his findings to the children. "Look what I found in her hand."

"Clue spray?" gawked Miriam. They all joined her laughter.

"I can't imagine how she planned to thwart her attackers with that, but I wouldn't put it past her," Sir Peter declared. "Now not a word of it to your father."

They all agreed but couldn't wait to tell Musa and Kubri. Miriam and Grandpa Baul approached the driver to explain they would be loading a sick patient onboard before Mrs. Baul was hauled into view. He readily agreed to take them past the hot springs on their way back. It was less than a mile away. Once there, Lady Sarah donned gloves to inspect the bird and immediately noticed its wing had been broken, no need to do further tests. Miriam didn't want the vultures to eat it so she reverently buried it in a grave of loose sand.

"We need to get Mrs. Baul back to the lodge before she wakes up," explained Lady Sarah.

"Will she remember what happened?" asked Joe.

"She won't know we were involved that's for sure," said Sir Peter. "We've given her a small memory block assister as well so she doesn't pursue any bad nightmares of her desert adventure."

"How soon until Kubri and Rev. Baul's rendezvous?" asked Lady Sarah.

"Haj Sayed promised to meet them just after sundown," said Grandpa Baul.

"Grandpa, can we do some more sand boarding?" asked Joe.

"Please?" joined in Miriam. "You haven't tried out the sledding yet."

"Well, we can't do it with your mom in her present condition," said Grandpa. "There would be no explaining that to the driver."

"Why don't you drop the doctors and patient back at the lodge and then head out for another spin?" suggested Sir Peter.

"I suppose it wouldn't hurt," said Grandpa. "But we wouldn't be able to see very well. It's getting dark and there's not much of a moon out tonight."

"We could use our night vision goggles!" Joe beamed.

"Yeah!" said Miriam. "Great idea, Joe."

"Well, why not?" decided Grandpa. "As long as we're back in time to hear about the meeting with Haj Sayed."

"Done," announced Sir Peter. "We'll stay in phone contact and Musa will still be glued in position. He's going to need a vacation once this all blows over."

"That's for sure," said Lady Sarah. "Maybe he'll want to float us down the Nile again, Peter?"

"We'll see."

The ride back to town went quickly. Thankfully they found their arrival at the lodge unobserved, as sunset drinks were entertaining the other guests on the rooftop. Musa and Kubri ran out to greet them and Mrs. Baul was comfortably installed in her room. The eager sand boarders hopped back in the jeep and dropped Kubri off at the pigeon race center so he could break the good news of Mrs. Baul's safety to his friend before walking over to their meeting.

-23-

News of Bishop Edwin

"Cornwall?"

"Baul?"

"You're alive?" Rev. Baul grabbed his old schoolmate and embraced him unabashedly. "*Al hamdulillah*! Thanks be to God!"

Haj Sayed and Kubri looked on with great celebration, echoing identical sentiments.

"How did you find him, Haj Sayed?" exclaimed Kubri.

"You will not believe my story," Haj Sayed announced, his face shining with relief and delight. "I will give you time with your friend to hear his version, and then you will hear mine."

"It really is you!" Rev. Baul could hardly believe it. "Are you injured in any way?"

"Never been better," the Rt. Rev. Edwin Cornwall-McGrath III declared with a sincere twinkle in his eye. Although his build was slight, his presence was most imposing.

"My new friends," began Haj Sayed, "Before we reveal all the details of this remarkable mystery, I insist you accept my invitation for your family and friends to be my honored guests this evening."

"How can we refuse?" beamed Rev. Baul. "But at such late notice, your wife will be most upset won't she?"

"My wife will welcome you as if nobility," said Haj Sayed. "Our village will join in the festivities and preparation. I will pick you up in two hours."

"We are honored," Kubri spoke their gratitude.

Neither Kubri nor Rev. Baul could wait for the details and began probing the bishop for his side of the story. He assured them it was neither heroic nor dramatic but they insisted they couldn't wait for the others. Kubri paused to call lodge headquarters and cheering could be heard in the background. Rev. Baul immediately placed a call to Bishop Kareem who was overwhelmed with joy. He would notify the archbishop and draft a general press release, but wait for further details promised within the hour.

"Before we go one more step, Cornwall, you must ring your mother in London," Rev. Baul would not take no for an answer.

As they listened to the bishop assure his mother of his safety they could only imagine the delightful gift she was receiving. Her phones had been tapped by MI6 and by the time the three men arrived at the lodge, a swarm of reporters was waiting. The tall dark frame of Musa welcomed them, huge white teeth spread against the dark of the night. Sir Peter managed to clear the way through on the grounds that a short statement to the press would be made before dinner.

Kubri thanked the lodge manager for his efforts that day and promised to fill him in on the full details later. His final request was for riders to be sent to retrieve their three camels, visible from the cold spring yet not far from what they discovered was the well-known Bir Wahid, hot springs. The manager assured him a jeep would be dispatched immediately with suitable riders onboard.

Promised a hot shower and rest before dinner, the bishop retired to his room. Kubri and Rev. Baul were eager to pass on the story to the others.

"Hello, Dad?" Rev. Baul was delighted to be the one to break the good news to his father.

"Son!" shouted Grandpa Baul. "Your children have turned me into a sledding sandman." Laughter and shouting could be heard in the background. The night vision sand boarding had clearly been a success.

"He's safe! The bishop is safe!" Rev. Baul shouted back.

"He's alive?" asked Grandpa Baul for confirmation. The known details were relayed in short and Grandpa Baul cheered the announcement. Signaling Miriam and Joe with the news he signed off with the promise to head back and celebrate.

"Now where is my lovely wife?" Rev. Baul asked the others.

"Right this way, she is asking for you," Sir Peter led his friend down the corridor to his room and found Lady Sarah fusing over Rev. Baul's wife.

Mrs. Baul looked a bit drowsy but glowing with happiness when she saw her handsome husband enter the room.

"Darling, are you okay?" she asked first.

"I'm fine my love, what about you?" Rev. Baul took her tenderly in his arms and Sir Peter and Lady Sarah slipped out the door with promises to catch up over dinner.

Tech headquarters sprang to life again when Grandpa and the children marched through the door. Still shaking sand from their hair and clothes, they were treated to the details of the missing bishop's rescue, and assured of the full version over dinner with Haj Sayed and his villagers. No one could believe things had turned out as they had.

"I assure you all that the incident has been explained to Mrs. Baul so that Rev. Baul won't worry or probe more than is necessary," Lady Sarah reported. "The gaps in her memory were revealed in her questions but she seemed satisfied with the details she was given."

"What did she say when she found out Madame Napoleon had been whisked off to Cairo?" asked Grandpa Baul.

"It was most upsetting news to be sure," Lady Sarah admitted. "But an exact timeframe did not seem important in light of the discovery of the bishop. In truth, without her valiant adventuresome desert forays, the mystery of his disappearance would not have been pursued."

"Ironic isn't it?" declared Sir Peter.

Mrs. Baul's presence was requested at the formal press conference but the group voted that Rev. Baul read the statement. The Right Reverend joined them to pose for the eager photographers and graciously shook the hands of many present. When the bishop reached Rev. Baul's stalking journalist, the "nuke watchdog" reporter turned in his direction and nodded a sign of satisfaction. His knowing gaze caught the eye of both Musa and Kubri.

"Hey Kubri, that guy shaking the bishop's hand is the same guy we saw in El-Dabaa," whispered Musa loudly.

"He sure is," confirmed Kubri. "I can't believe this is the guy who's been hounding Rev. Baul."

"I can't either," agreed Musa. "Should we confront him?"

"Let's just see how things play out," suggested Kubri. "It sounds like he's come around to some form of honesty with Rev. Baul at least."

"True," he said, calming down quickly.

"Haj Sayed's entourage has arrived to take you to dinner," announced the lodge manager at just the opportune moment. "Thank you for joining us ladies and gentlemen. A lavish Siwan buffet dinner can be found on the rooftop for all ecolodge guests."

The group dispersed reluctantly and the Bauls made their way to the front of the lodge. Three spectacular carriages drawn by beautiful white Arabian stallions stood awaiting their arrival. Haj Sayed waved to them in welcome and asked Mrs. Baul and Lady Sarah to join him in the front carriage. After all Mrs. Baul had been through her first instinct was instant distrust but she quickly checked herself, not wanting to let Lady Sarah sense her apprehension. The bishop helped them in and rode with them as well for the journey. The Radcliffes had been acquainted with Bishop Edwin during their Cambridge days, so the recent reunion had been a happy one indeed.

Rev. Baul and Sir Peter broke into wide smiles and joined the others. Kubri and Musa rode with Rev. Baul who launched into an intense discussion on pigeon racing strategies now that the worry about his wife and the missing bishop was behind him. Her proud grandfather helped a beautiful Miriam into the final carriage while Sir Peter and his godson claimed the rear seats.

"I would like to welcome our honored guests formally to our village," announced Haj Sayed for all to hear. "They have come a great distance to join us and we are grateful for their presence with us."

"On behalf of my fellow countrymen," began Bishop Edwin, "I want to thank Siwa for all the gracious hospitality shown. It is a memory I will never forget."

Dinner was served, and breaking with tradition, Haj Sayed placed both genders of his visiting guests at his own expansive low sitting table. An elaborate spread of appetizers greeted their hungry appetites: grapevine leaves stuffed with spiced rice, *baba ghannoug*, made from eggplant, and *hummous*, a chickpea dip all to accompany delicious flat bread, fresh from the outdoor brick oven.

Rev. Baul was especially happy to hear the restful sounds of an Oud playing in the background. Hand-woven camel wool carpets and pillows lined the floor of the outdoor dining room. Stars pierced the silent darkness decorating the sky as tall flaming torches competed to provide light of pure palm oil that would burn late into the night.

"Now, my friends. To the story of rescue," began Haj Sayed nodding his head in deference toward the bishop. "I know you have probably heard the missing bishop's version but mine must be told as well."

Haj Sayed commenced an elaborate retelling of his journey to interrupt the annual desert retreat. He had chosen camelback as a less threatening mode of transportation than a motor vehicle to ensure he was not mistaken for a wandering traveler or tourist police. Upon arrival, in light of the reported state of emergency his ceremonial request to be taken to the head sheikh's tent was immediately granted.

"When I entered the good sheikh's tent quarters, whom did I find but a foreigner being hosted with great pomp and ceremony. Eating choice dates and sipping our *karkade* I found this man entertaining the sheikh's own grandson in English. It was none other than the Rt. Rev. Edwin Cornwall-McGrath III!" Haj Sayed paused to savor his story.

"You can imagine my surprise to find that nothing seemed awry. I explained to the sheikh the dire consequences of this international situation and the grave repercussions this hostage taking could evoke. At that point our dear bishop launched into dialogue with me in English, which initially made the sheikh nervous. But the nodding head of his grandson assured him there was no deception underway." At this point in the story Haj Sayed requested that the bishop pick up the narrative.

"Well, as you can imagine I was shocked to hear I was missing!" announced the bishop. "I had hired a driver for a bit of dune riding for the day and our car broke down and was claimed to be irreparable. The driver brought me here to the encampment to shelter me. He warned me that no one was ever allowed to interrupt the retreat. I didn't really know what choice I had, but the minute the young boys saw a European, they all dashed over to practice their English."

"So what happened to the jeep and driver, sir?" interrupted Joe.

"He was loaned a camel by the retreat organizers and I never heard from him again," explained the bishop. "I figured it could take quite a few days to sort out the jeep repairs and retrieve me. I really was in no hurry to get back as I had been so warmly welcomed and it became for me a holiday adventure. The character of these young men who were learning the ways of their elders impressed me, as did their abilities in English."

"We have found the jeep driver," continue Haj Sayed. "A well intentioned hard working man, yet a little embarrassed to have violated a well known taboo, so to speak. He was still here in town collecting supplies but never guessed the rumor of a missing churchman in Libya had any relation to him."

After a moment, Kubri expressed gratefulness on behalf of the group. "For your warm and generous hospitality we thank you."

-24-

Racing terrorists home

Mrs. Baul was awaked from a deep sleep by the sound of her husband's alarm clock. No sign of light could be seen through the crack in their palm frond shutters.

"You brought along that miserable clock?" she said groggily, exhausted and terribly sore. Her dreams had been tortured renditions of bishops on camelback fighting armed donkeys with nuclear weapons, Bedouin sheikhs stockpiling Oud-shaped missiles and half buried red jeeps.

"I'm sorry, my love," her husband said soothingly. "It was the only way I would get up in time for the pigeon race liftoff."

"Why so early?" she complained.

"I've got to tend to them first thing this morning and get them comfortable in their carrying case before release time arrives," he explained apologetically.

"Of course, I forgot. I'm sorry sweetheart. Yesterday is a blur. Did we really find the kidnapped bishop?" she asked.

"Safe and well, thank goodness."

"And Madame Napoleon?" Mrs. Baul was still worried about her dear friend.

"Her husband is with her at the hospital in Cairo. She is going to be fine."

"Can I have ten more minutes?" she begged sleepily.

"Definitely," Rev. Baul tucked the covers up over her shoulders and headed off to get ready.

The Baul party of men had signed up for the first carload to leave for the pigeon race. Sensibly the women voted for sleep, accepting the kind offer that Musa's driver would shuttle them over to the race station just before the competition was scheduled to start. All agreed to return for a leisurely breakfast with the bishop after the event was underway.

"Don't they look eager?" smiled Rev. Baul as he reveled in the sounds of flapping wings and cooing birds.

"They look prepared to beat us back to Cairo," confirmed Musa.

Many pigeon fanciers worked to perfect widowhood racing techniques to increase speed and loft loyalty. One mate would remain back at the home dovecote and only ever be allowed to see his or her companion fifteen minutes before and after a race. Consistent with his character, Rev. Baul projected his human kindness onto the pigeons he nurtured and refused to practice such methods. He saw his flying friends as servants of mankind and loved to tell stories of the noble history of their breed. He admired their superb athleticism, strong determination and loyalty to their home lofts and owners.

Instead of widowhood, Rev. Baul and Musa had worked out a system to release the hen first and then let the cock follow shortly in pursuit. Their most impressive performances had happened when nesting instincts were heightened and recently weaned babies awaited them at home. That was the case with these two young birds. They had the best chance possible to race successfully.

"Cinnamon! Sugar!" called Miriam as she ran from the car toward her father.

"Miriam!" called Rev. Baul with a bright smile of welcome. "Here they are. They're happy and ready for action."

"You made it, my love!" exclaimed Rev. Baul eagerly when he spotted his wife hurrying ahead of Lady Sarah. "Come stand by my side. Watch your step, ladies."

"Isn't this exciting?" said Mrs. Baul eagerly embracing the moment. "Do you really think they'll make it back home, dear?"

"I do," said her husband. "Musa has trained them well. We only can hone the instincts they've already been given."

"Well it certainly would be a memorable occasion," said Mrs. Baul. "Can your office walls even hold more winning certificates?"

"Musa has plenty of room on his sailboat," smiled Rev. Baul before changing the subject. "See that man over there? He is the one who let the pigeons loose to give himself an advantage in the race."

"Really? How shocking," exclaimed Mrs. Baul. "Has he been punished?"

"Yes, he's been banned from the race," he replied. "That kind of sabotage won't be forgotten by the other pigeon fanciers."

"It's probably hit the pigeon network back in Cairo by now," added Musa.

"I wouldn't be surprised," agreed Rev. Baul. "Watch the clock now, we're almost ready to go."

"How long do you think it will take them to get home?" asked Joe.

"Musa, what do you think?" asked Rev. Baul.

"Why don't we each make a guess?" suggested Miriam. "You go first Dad."

"Let's see, 350 miles. I'll say nine hours," decided her father.

"I'll go with six and a half," braved Musa.

The remaining predictions fell in between the two respected opinions. Soon the race secretary officially announced confirmation that the weather conditions were favorable; the feathered athletes awaited release.

"Look at them go!" cried Lady Sarah a moment later. "They're so graceful and dramatic."

After liberation, all the birds flew off together before the leader birds lofted and broke away. It was a breathtaking sight.

"This is truly remarkable," Kubri exclaimed. "I've never seen anything like it."

"I'm so glad you've joined us," Rev. Baul said appreciatively as he proudly watched his birds fade into the distance, desperately hoping they'd find their way home.

The Rt. Rev. Edwin Cornwall-McGrath III awoke refreshed from a dream and found Egypt's sun warming his face. It took him a moment to reorient himself, but soon he remembered the weeping voice of his mother, joyful beyond description. His hospitable hosts and his fervent rescuers had shown him such kindness. What a holiday. He would miss his new friends. His world had expanded quite suddenly. Expecting an onslaught of journalists, he waited for the knock promised by his friend.

"Cornwall? Baul here," called his friend's voice from the hallway.

"Good morning," answered the bishop as he swung the door open. "How did the race liftoff go?"

"Perfect. Beautiful morning and the birds were all in good form."

"Glad to hear it. Wish I could have gotten myself up that early. I'm still feeling a bit disoriented. That's quite a hobby you have going there, Baul."

"I do enjoy it," admitted Rev. Baul. "Something completely different from parish responsibilities. You remember those days?"

"Yes, there is stress in all walks of life, though, to be sure," he replied. "It's good to find diversions from daily responsibilities. You certainly have a good family and group of friends behind you. That surely makes life more enjoyable."

"I'm very grateful," said Rev. Baul before refocusing on the day ahead. "Ready for breakfast? I'm your escort through the relentless crowd of cameras."

"Thank you. I'm famished."

At the insistence of the lodge manager the Baul entourage was given a private dining space for their meal. Arrangements had been made for a larger aircraft so the whole crew could join the Bauls on the return journey to Cairo. Musa's hired driver would head back shortly with a couple young journalists who needed a ride.

Rev. Baul had spoken again with Bishop Kareem back in Cairo who was insisting on hosting his fellow bishop for the night at his cathedral guesthouse. He would then fly back to London first thing the next morning. The Archbishop of

Canterbury had scheduled a meeting for a full debriefing in cooperation with MI6. Even with such a happy ending to the mishap it was imperative that details be gathered to prevent such an unnecessary international incident in the future. Once those responsibilities were cared for, the bishop's request to take his vacation with his mother on the coast of Wales would be granted.

Sir Peter and Lady Sarah eagerly accepted the invitation to stay on with the Bauls for a weeklong visit. Kubri and Musa had volunteered to stand watch at the home pigeon coop that evening while the others went to the weekly church service, but after making a hospital visit. Mrs. Baul was very apologetic when pressed into admitting that her suspicions of weapons of mass destruction had been erroneous. But she did point out that Madame Napoleon's experience with the "terrorists" stalking her still needed controlling, and quickly.

Leaving Siwa after such a whirlwind emotion filled visit seemed a bit abrupt to all. The hotel manager sent them on their way with a warm invitation to return soon. When the departing entourage arrived at the Siwa airstrip field, Haj Sayed emerged from a waiting car to send them off with a blessing.

"Thank you all for honoring our village with your presence as our guests last night," Haj Sayed's heartfelt expression began. "May God's peace be upon each of you now and always."

"And may God's peace bless you and your loved ones Haj Sayed," Rev. Baul graciously offered on behalf of the others.

Upon arrival in Cairo, the passengers could see a swarm of journalists attempting to get near their airplane. Security lines were quickly enforced, compliments of Kubri's cousin and in coordination with a British Embassy security detail. Debriefing at Bishop Edwin's home embassy would precede his being taken to the cathedral grounds. It would be up to the British Embassy to coordinate another official statement concerning the incident.

The press was held back at a distance, but Mrs. Baul turned her head in surprise when she heard her name called loudly from the crowd, demanding an interview. Grandpa Baul locked eyes with Kubri in a silent pact of understanding. No interviews would be given by Mrs. Baul.

As Madame Napoleon's hospital was not far from the airport it seemed logical to stop there first for a visit. Most of the group stayed in the hospital waiting room while Rev. and Mrs. Baul went to talk briefly with her.

"My friend!" exclaimed Madame Napoleon. "You are alive! You have come back!"

"We found the kidnapped bishop," she explained. "I will give you every possible detail once you are up to coffee at our café again. How are you feeling?"

"I'm just fine, thank you. My husband told me the bishop had been found, but never really had been kidnapped?"

"Well, it was all one big mix-up," Mrs. Baul continued. "You know how these things can happen. Remember our misgivings about Kubri and the donkey rescue and the weapons of mass destruction?"

"Did you find the missing clues?" asked Madame Napoleon.

"Our inklings were false," she stated with a hint of regret. "This time."

"Dear Madame Napoleon," Rev. Baul decided enough had been said on the subject for now. "It is so good to see you in much better health. We were very worried about you."

"Thank you," she smiled, as her husband came to her side.

"Thank you for all your help in the emergency, Rev. Baul," declared her husband. "The doctors believe it was a severe food poisoning for she has continued to heal once those symptoms were treated. Her eye infection cleared up rapidly, its presence just a coincidence. They definitely expect the lab tests will confirm the food poisoning diagnosis so she is free to go home as soon as her strength returns."

"It was our pleasure to be able to help," confirmed Rev. Baul.

"The terrorists! Watch out!" Madame Napoleon shrieked as she saw Kubri and Musa appear at her door.

"No, my dear," explained Mrs. Baul. "Everything is okay. I asked them to come along to see you. They are not terrorists. They've proven themselves close and trusted friends. We would not have found the missing bishop without their valuable help."

"Madame Napoleon, Monsieur Napoleon," both men nodded as they entered the room and shook hands warmly with them both.

"Really?" exclaimed Madame trying to laugh at herself. "What an error we made!"

"All is forgiven," assured Kubri.

"Innocent intentions," Musa added. "No permanent harm done."

Rev. Baul was still not entirely clear on all the facts and assumptions that were being talked about so nonchalantly. He had certainly missed something along the way. Madame

Napoleon's husband looked equally, if not more, confused. But as Rev. Baul saw his wife's cheerful smile he knew it was time to be celebrating. Her friend would recover and the bishop had been found. What more could he possibly ask for?

"We don't want to tire you out too much," said Mrs. Baul as she rose to leave. "I will visit you again in the morning. We're off to prepare for our Pentecost service."

"Thank you so much for everything," Madame Napoleon replied. "By the way, I had my driver drop off your new painting while you were gone."

"Painting?" asked Rev. Baul.

"*Gameelah,* my painting!" exclaimed Kubri with a knowing wink in the reverend's direction.

"I suppose there is still a bit more to explain," Mrs. Baul said with a wince.

"Not at all," declared Kubri. "I am honored that you could not resist one of my artistic endeavors."

-25-

The fate of Cinnamon and Sugar

As the organ filled their historic church with music that evening, Rev. Baul, his long white robe draped with a scarlet stole, began the processional down the aisle with Joseph and the other young acolytes symbolically leading the way east toward the altar. He smiled contentedly as he singled out his wife's and daughter's soprano voices in the choir. A dancing symphony of color caught his eye as he passed by the round windows overlooking the nave. His friend, the Muslim stained-glass window artist of Al-Azhar Mosque, had handcrafted them.

Both Bishop Kareem and Bishop Edwin had spontaneously appeared shortly before the service was due to begin, to bring ceremonial greetings from the Archbishop of Canterbury. Mrs. Baul's voice quivered momentarily when she spotted two newcomers, the Donkey Rescue president and his wife. Their presence confirmed her misplaced assumptions, but she reminded herself that her intentions had only arisen out of concern for the well being of others; well, that and perhaps an innate longing for a bit of adventure. There was the fear factor of course, but she'd be more careful next time.

Following the recessional hymn the little congregation gathered in the garden for the releasing of the dove. The youngest children were allowed to push forward to the front. Mrs. Baul caught her breath as her husband skillfully tossed the white winged bird high into the air. All heads arched back and watched the freed wings expand to full width, circle the garden once and gracefully soar off toward home. A contented smile appeared on Rev. Baul's face as he saw the children jumping up and down with animated joy.

Miriam and Joe raced the Pentecost pigeon back to the vicarage with Grandpa Baul, impatient to see if Cinnamon and Sugar had found their way home. To their dismay they discovered Musa and Kubri in the garden with solemn expressions. They were ignoring the recently returned white bird, which sat on the rim of the aviary.

"They didn't make it?" asked Grandpa Baul breathless from running.

"They did," said Musa breaking into a broad smile.

"They did?" yelled Miriam and Joe in confusion.

"Not twenty minutes ago!" declared Kubri standing to greet them.

"You guys!" threatened Miriam.

They all laughed at themselves and headed for a look at the winged travelers.

"Wow! They found their way home," Joe was impressed.

"I'm so happy they made it!" cheered Miriam.

"That was a long distance to fly for their first real test," Grandpa commented. "What was their arrival time?"

"Four thirty-three. Eight hours, thirty-three minutes and twelve seconds," Musa stated officially.

"Hey, Mom won the bet!" Miriam grinned.

"Not bad for their first race. There will be no time setting certificates coming our way, but we have lots of success to celebrate anyway," added Musa.

"I am amazed they could find their way home," said Kubri.

"They surely do look happy to see their babies," observed Miriam.

"Yes, they do," agreed Musa. "We'll have those babies out loft flying soon."

"Dad and Mom won't be here for a while because Bishop Edwin and Bishop Kareem showed up for the service," explained Joe.

"We're in no hurry," said Musa. "Our job is done. We've just been discussing Mrs. Baul in fact."

"Yes, my *Gameelah*," mused Kubri with a broad smile on his face. "What to do?"

"Any ideas on thwarting future imaginative adventure before it begins?" asked Musa.

"You know we've tried every angle imaginable," added Grandpa Baul.

"What about throwing her diaries into the Nile, Musa?" suggested Joe in jest.

"As if that would do a lot of good," Miriam added. "Remember her conclusions the last time they went missing?"

They all shook their heads and laughed. Within minutes cold lemonade and snacks were served in the garden. The household staff's break was short lived.

"*Shokran,* thank you," said Miriam. "What's for dinner tonight?"

"Rev. Baul's favorite," the answer was voiced with pride.

"You'll like this, Kubri," said Musa. "Guaranteed to be a West African spread, right kids?"

"None other," grinned Joe. "Dad's contacts keep importing the ingredients to make his favorite dishes."

"Only our trusted cook is allowed to touch his stockpile," added Miriam playfully.

Before long the pigeon reception committee was able to welcome the others returning from church. The news of the pigeons' successful flight was cheered and of course they all needed more details than just the time records.

"Who got here first?" asked Mrs. Baul impatiently.

"They both flew in together, but the hen, excuse me Miriam, Sugar, cleared the ace hole first," announced Musa. "Compliments of her doting mate."

"Well done," declared Rev. Baul. "Did you check them for scrapes or torn feathers?"

"All is well," assured Musa.

Everyone enjoyed the evening spent in the garden discussing the events of the week. It was hard to believe the children had to go to school the next morning. Peter and Sarah sketched rough plans for the week with every intention of keeping the Baul's normal routine intact. At Mrs. Baul's insistence they agreed to join the traveling medical clinic one day for a visit to the outskirts of Cairo. At the minimum they would all meet up for dinner each evening. One of Lady Sarah's priorities was to sail with Musa, after Mrs. Baul's requests of course, and Kubri insisted on hosting them one day for lunch after a personal tour of his gallery. Finally the group reluctantly parted ways, fatigue beginning to settle in.

The back of a large canvas caught Rev. Baul's eye as he escorted his wife into the house.

"What is this, my love?" he asked, feigning ignorance.

"Oh how delightful!" declared Mrs. Baul. "The donkey masterpiece Madame Napoleon sent over. Would you please put it up for me tonight?"

"Tonight?" he asked wearily.

"Please? I know you're tired and it's gotten late, but it would perfectly complete the week's venture," she persuaded.

As they were drifting off to sleep that night, Mrs. Baul whispered, "Sweetheart, what do you think of that gift Bishop Kareem presented to me tonight? I'm just wondering if there may be more to it than meets the eye?"